TOM AND HUCK'S
HOWLING ADVENTURE

This Large Print Book carries the
Seal of Approval of N.A.V.H.

ADVENTURES IN TIME—1849, BOOK ONE

TOM AND HUCK'S HOWLING ADVENTURE

THE FURTHER ADVENTURES OF TOM SAWYER AND HUCKLEBERRY FINN

TIM CHAMPLIN

WHEELER PUBLISHING
A part of Gale, a Cengage Company

GALE
A Cengage Company

Farmington Hills, Mich • San Francisco • New York • Waterville, Maine
Meriden, Conn • Mason, Ohio • Chicago

Copyright © 2017 by Tim Champlin.
Wheeler Publishing, a part of Gale, a Cengage Company.

Wheeler Publishing Large Print Western.
The text of this Large Print edition is unabridged.
Other aspects of the book may vary from the original edition.
Set in 16 pt. Plantin.

LIBRARY OF CONGRESS CIP DATA ON FILE.
CATALOGUING IN PUBLICATION FOR THIS BOOK
IS AVAILABLE FROM THE LIBRARY OF CONGRESS

ISBN-13: 978-1-4104-9697-3 (softcover)

Published in 2018 by arrangement with Tim Champlin

Printed in Mexico
1 2 3 4 5 6 7 22 21 20 19 18

For my daughter, Liz,
with all my Love
and Admiration

FOREWORD

Tim Champlin has succeeded where Mark Twain failed. Mark Twain tried several times to write successful sequels to *Adventures of Huckleberry Finn,* but for various reasons he could not finish them or they did not succeed when they were published.

In 1884, the year *Huckleberry Finn* was published, Twain began writing "Huck Finn and Tom Sawyer Among the Indians," starting the action where *Huckleberry Finn* ends, but for some reason he gave it up after writing more than 200 pages of manuscript. It centers around a kidnapping, and features some western scenes and gruesome events, but Twain gave up the idea without figuring out what would happen next. It remained unpublished until 1968.

In 1892 he wrote *Tom Sawyer Abroad,* which was published as a book in 1894, and although it begins shortly after *Huckleberry Finn* ends, it's not really a sequel and was not successful. In this tale, Tom, Huck, Jim, and a mad professor float across the Atlantic Ocean toward Africa in a balloon. The mad professor falls overboard along the way, and the story soon ends in Africa. A lot of other things happen, but there's hardly a plot — just a lot of action that leads nowhere.

The same year *Tom Sawyer Abroad* was published, Twain wrote another sequel, *Tom Sawyer, Detective,* which was published in book form in 1896. This story centers around a murder mystery and includes a lot of action that resembles Tom and Huck's original adventures. Much of the action takes place along the Mississippi River in the same places as their original adventures. The tale ends in a dramatic trial with Tom and Huck splitting a reward like they did in *The Adventures of Tom Sawyer,* and although this story was indeed a sequel to Twain's original story, it also met with little success.

The year after *Tom Sawyer, Detective* was published, Twain wrote a sequel to that work called "Tom Sawyer's Conspiracy," but it remained unfinished like his first attempt and was not published until 1969. In this story Tom and Huck decide to pull a hoax on their village, but are instead swept up into a murder for which their friend Jim is falsely accused. The story takes place along the Mississippi River and includes some characters from their original adventures, and it also ends in a dramatic trial. There are scattered notes for other stories about Tom and Huck that Twain planned, but he never figured out exactly what to do with his two most famous characters after their famous adventures came to a conclusion at the end of *Huckleberry Finn.*

But Tim Champlin is not Mark Twain. Tim picks up where Twain left off, and knows exactly what to do, and the result is a page-turner that includes kidnappings, chase scenes, steamboats, gold treasure, a tornado, mystery, guns, knives, close calls, a wagon train, Indians, time travel, a girl who discovers she is tougher than she thought, and a boy who learns about modern life from the past in unexpected ways. Twain himself wrote other stories that include all of these things. In fact, his own attempts at sequels to *Huckleberry Finn* include most of these elements, and his 1889 book, *A Connecticut Yankee in King Arthur's Court,* features time travel. But Twain never managed to fit all of them into one of his failed sequels to his world-famous masterpiece.

At the end of *Tom Sawyer,* Tom and Huck split a $12,000 reward, and at the end of *Huckleberry Finn,* Huck decides he must light out for the territory. At the beginning of Tim's tale, Tom and Huck are planning to do just that, and are about to ask Jim to join them in their scheme when events take an unexpected turn. Before they can act on their desire for more adventures, they meet somebody from the future who surprises them as much as they surprise him. Then someone dear to them goes missing, and the adventures begin. Tim's themes are Twain's themes, and Tim's locales are Twain's locales, and Tom, Huck, Jim, and others speak authentically, just as they did in Twain's original tale. Their adventures are a logical extension of their earlier adventures — a true sequel. Many others have tried to bring Tom and Huck back to life in the more than one hundred years since Twain's last failed attempt, but none have succeeded until now. More could be said, but why spoil the surprises and the fun? What are you waiting for? You've got a book full of pages in your hand waiting to be turned.

Kevin Mac Donnell,
Mark Twain Journal Legacy Scholar
Austin, Texas

"And then Tom he talked along and talked along, and says, le's all three slide out of here one of these nights and get an outfit, and go for howling adventures amongst the Injuns, over in the Territory, for a couple of weeks or two; and I says, all right that suits me, but I ain't got no money for to buy the outfit, and I reckon I couldn't get none from home, because it's likely pap's been back before now and got it all away from Judge Thatcher and drunk it up.

" 'No, he hain't,' Tom says; 'it's all there yet — six thousand dollars and more; and your pap hain't ever been back since. Hadn't when I come away, anyhow.' "

—from the conclusion of
Adventures of Huckleberry Finn
by Mark Twain

CHAPTER 1

Monday, June 4, 1849
St. Petersburg, Missouri

The dusty village on the west bank of the Mississippi was about to explode, but nobody knew it.

Least of all did Tom Sawyer know it, concerned only with his personal explosion of joy and relief that long-awaited summer vacation had arrived.

Wiping the last of the sticky jam from his mouth with a sleeve, he stepped out the front door of the two-story white frame house where he lived with his Aunt Polly, older cousin, Mary, and half-brother, Sid. He paused and surveyed his domain, which consisted of the broad street and three or four buildings a half block in either direction. The whole world lay at his feet, and his head was bursting with possibilities.

How to fill this first wonderful day of summer — swimming, fishing, kite flying, marbles, hoops? Naw! All that was child's play, fine when he was younger, but he'd been through some mighty adventures these past two summers — enough for most boys to brag about for years. Yet, at thirteen and a half years old, he wasn't satisfied — only poisoned for more.

His pirate gang had fallen apart, due mostly to grown-up restrictions on robbery and murder. But that was simply make-believe, anyhow, with wooden swords and secret blood oaths. He was grown up now. And, as the Good Book said, "When I became a man, I put away childish things."

Stepping off the plank sidewalk, he took a deep breath of fresh air. None of his friends was in sight. Following the path of least resistance, he gravitated downhill toward the river a block away, feeling the cool cobblestones under his feet, the callused soles not yet leather-tough.

It was time to pick up where he'd left off at the end of last summer's adventure on the Phelps farm down in Arkansas. He'd been fired up to continue their adventures by lighting out for the territory with Huck and Jim.

But the bullet wound in his own leg had prevented it. Instead, limping with a bandaged calf, he'd returned north on a steamboat to St. Petersburg with Huck and Jim and Aunt Polly. For two or three delicious weeks, he and Huck and Jim had been praised and honored as returning heroes, fawned over, written about in the newspaper, forced to tell their story over and over to eager ears.

Tom gloried in the other boys' wide-eyed hero worship, their secret envy, and the girls' admiring glances. Continuing a slight limp long after it was necessary, he wore ragged pants cut off at the knee to exhibit the scar. And the grandest moment of all was when he showed off the lead bullet he wore around his neck on an old watch fob.

Blacks gathered from far and near to hear Jim's tale. Wild as his story was, he made his adventures better with each retelling, tossing in witches to account for being lost in the fog, for turning him into a blue-faced A-rab to scare strangers, for the sudden explosion of rats in his prison cabin.

Now a free man, Jim had commenced working for the Widow Douglas for wages, vowing to buy his wife and children out of bondage "if it takes a hundert years."

"Hey, Tom!"

The hail broke his reverie as Huck Finn approached from the foot of Cardiff Hill.

"Hey, yourself. Where you headed?" It

pained him to see Huck dressed in a clean cotton shirt and pants that were a decent fit. And his hair had been recently trimmed! Life at the widow's was taking its toll on his old friend. But he didn't feel so bad when Huck, with a glance over his shoulder, pulled a pipe from his pocket and stuck the stem between his teeth without filling or lighting it. Huck had also shucked his shoe leather.

The boys fell into step continuing toward the river landing another block south.

"The *Annabelle* is due down from Keokuk, this mornin'," Huck said. "Reckon I'll go see if anybody's comin' ashore here."

"If they is, 'tain't likely nobody we know," Tom said. But watching a steamboat land and discharge freight and passengers was always an exciting spectacle.

The boys seated themselves on a stack of boxes above the sloping cobblestone landing, staring out at the mass of green water sliding past fifty feet away. Huck pulled out a leaf of limp, half-cured tobacco and began shredding it to pack his pipe.

Tom fingered the lead bullet hanging from his neck. Its charm had fled, vanishing with their brief glory and fame months ago.

"Huck, 'member when we come home last summer as heroes?"

"Yeah. That was a fine time."

"But it didn't last."

"Nothin' ever does."

"Do you miss the old days before we was famous?"

"Maybe a little. But I didn't scarcely have enough to eat then. Now there's plenty, even if I have to say grace over it all the time and use a knife and fork and napkin and all them things." He paused with a faraway look as if recalling events of long ago. "Sleeping in the woods or a hogshead is fine in warm weather. But come winter, not even the old tannery or a hayloft can shut out the cold. These here clothes like to smother me, but I reckon there's always a price to pay."

"So you're sayin' you like it at the widow's better than when you was free?"

Huck didn't reply for a few seconds as he struck a lucifer and puffed his pipe to life.

"Wal, things ain't *all* bad. The widow's old maid sister, Miss Watson, is dead and gone so she ain't peckin' at me no more. And the widow she lets up on me now and again when she sees things is scrapin' too rough. I reckon it's like drippin' a tiny dose o'castor oil on your tongue every day 'til, by 'n' by, it don't taste too bad. I can still cuss and smoke if I go off by myself to do it.

17

Take it all around, I do miss my freedom, but I reckon I had enough o' that other life."

Tom's stomach felt as if he'd swallowed a lead sinker. What he'd feared most was coming to pass — Huck Finn was becoming respectable. There would soon be nobody the boys could look up to and envy.

"And, o' course Jim's there most o' the time to talk over old times with," Huck continued. "And you're here." He leaned his elbows on his knees and puffed, staring out over the vast sweep of water. The cool breeze whisked the pipe smoke away. "I figure we have 'most everythin' we could ever want," Huck continued, stretching his arms wide. "Each of us owns a pile o' gold worth more 'an six thousand dollars from that treasure, Injun Joe's dead, Pap's dead, you was able to set Muff Potter free from that murder charge, Miss Watson give Jim his freedom in her will, and we had some mighty fine times along the way whilst all them things was happenin'." He paused to tamp the fire in the corncob bowl with the head of a square nail. "Even school's tole'ble, I reckon. Switchin' don't mean shucks after the beatings Pap give me. And I'm learnin' to write a fair hand, and cipher and been discoverin' lots o' stuff about kings and revolutions and such I never knowed before."

Tom sunk further inside himself at this. A few seconds later, he mustered up strength to say, "Huck, are you sayin' you're done with havin' adventures for the rest of your life?"

"Wal . . . no, I reckon not. But I can't think o' nothin' right now we ain't done already."

"Don't you recollect what we talked about last summer down on the Phelps farm?"

"What's that?"

"Lighting out for new adventures in the territory amongst the Injuns and all that. And you said you was agreeable, but didn't have no money to buy an outfit because you figured your pap had come back here and got it all away from Judge Thatcher and drunk it up."

"Yeah, I do sorta recollect that."

"Well, are you still ready to go?"

"Hmm . . ."

"What else you fixin' to do all summer?" Tom insisted. "We'll grab Jim and use some of our money to buy horses and gear and we'll just haul off and *go.*"

"Tom, you know I always been up for trying 'most anything you come up with, 'cepten for that crazy stuff like goin' on a crusade and choppin' off folks' heads and

19

all that."

"No, no. I'm talking about a real grown-up adventure this time. If we like it well enough the first week or two, we can head farther west. I s'pect nearly half this village has already traipsed off toward California, chasin' gold. To keep it from being too dangersome, we could hook up with a wagon train for safety. They say they's herds of buffalo stretchin' as far as you can see. And those wild Plains Injuns . . . Well, no telling what else we'd see or what could happen."

"You know your Aunt Polly ain't gonna let you do nothin' o' the kind."

"I ain't gonna *ask* her. I'll leave her a note."

"Sid would find out and tell her sure."

"I'd bust his head if he did."

"And the widow, she ain't gonna let Jim take off on some wild trip like that."

"Jim's free. He can do what he wants."

"But he wants to keep workin' so's to buy his wife and children out of slavery."

"Huck, you and me both know Jim ain't gonna live long enough to do that with the wages he's earnin'."

"How much money d'ya reckon it'd take to buy Jim's family?" Huck wondered, staring off across the river. "We oughta dig into our pile o' gold to help him."

"Sure enough. I was thinkin' the same. We can slip around and find out how much a mother and two little kids is sellin' for these days. But we can't let on we want to buy 'em or their owner'll boost up the price."

"Yeah, and we'd best not tell Jim 'til they're free, in case sumpin' goes wrong," Huck cautioned. "Could be Providence will detour another direction."

"That's it! We could surprise him when we're all back home from the territory," Tom said, warming to his subject. "It'll be the best thing that ever happened to Jim — besides gettin' his *own* freedom." But then Tom had a better idea. "Looky here, if I can't convince Jim to go, I'll use that for the clincher. We'll promise to buy his family if he goes with us to the territory."

"You're talkin' like we already decided to go," Huck said. "Even if Jim wants to go — which he won't — the widow, she ain't gonna turn *me* loose. I reckon I'm in her charge now, and obliged to do what she says."

Tom ignored this comment and plunged ahead. "Maybe we could roust up Joe Harper and Ben Rogers to come along, too."

But Huck shook his head. "Their folks is even tougher than your Aunt Polly."

"Huck Finn, I don't know what to think

21

of such a sap-headed fool. Ain't you pos-
sessed of no gumption at'all? You used to
do whatever took your fancy, and was game
for any new enterprise. Now you're talkin'
like half the remainders of the folks in this
one-horse village who act like they're
hitched to singletrees and horse collars."

"And what about Becky Thatcher?"

"What about her?"

"I thought you was sweet on her."

"Girls come and go." He squirmed a bit
as an early pang of loneliness stabbed his
innards. "Anyways, she ain't gonna be
around. Her father's taking her down to
visit her cousins in Marsville for three
weeks. She ain't comin' back 'til the fourth
of July. You think I'm gonna sit around here
wastin' vacation while she's off havin' a lar-
rupin' good time? Not by a durn sight. I
got better things to do. She'll be mighty
proud o' me when I come back the end of
summer brown as an Injun, feathers in my
long hair, speakin' Sioux, wearin' buckskin
britches like a mountain man . . ."

"We been heroes before, you recollect, and
it didn't last no time."

"That's what living a life of adventure is
all about," Tom said, struggling to hold onto
his patience. "It don't stop. New things all
the time. If you quit and sit down, you go

22

to seed and before you can spit, you die. You want that?"

"Don't reckon I do."

"Well, then, let's snag Jim and bring some fishin' lines and go over to Jackson's Island and talk it over. If he's agreeable to go, it'd be good to have him along 'cause he's a full-grown man, and plenty strong in case o' trouble. And a nigger'd be an almighty curiosity amongst them Injuns who likely ain't never seen one before."

Huck drew on his pipe, discovered the fire was dead, and tapped out the dottle on a paving stone.

"I'm agreeable. We need a boat to row over t' the island."

"Go roust out Jim and I'll borrow one. One of these days I'm gonna buy one."

"Reckon it'd be good to have a skiff if we're gonna do much fishin' this summer," Huck said. "The widow says 'borrowing' ain't nothin' but a soft word for stealin' anyhow. How's a body supposed to feel when he has enough gold to waller in? Somehow I don't feel no different, even though I could buy a boat or anything else I want."

"We don't *have* all the money we want," Tom corrected him. "We can only lay our hands on whatever interest that money earns — about a dollar a day last I looked."

"Well, that's enough for me," Huck said. "Don't reckon I have that much to buy, nowadays, but maybe some fish hooks or tobacco."

"We'll have to talk the judge into dippin' into our gold if we buy horses and outfits," Tom said.

"How you gonna do that if you want t' keep this all a secret?" Huck asked.

"I'll make up some kind o' story to tell him," Tom said.

"Yeah. I learnt about dealin' with grown-ups when me and Jim was on the river," Huck said. "Mostly, I trusted to Providence to put the right words in my mouth when I needed 'em to keep us outa trouble. But I warn't as smart about that the year before when we found the gold. Now I look back on it, maybe we shoulda kept it all a dark secret, not told nobody and hid it somers so we could spend as much as we wanted on anything we had a mind to."

"Comes o' living with tethers on us," Tom said, a little sadly. "I hope you ain't discovered that too late."

As the boys left the levee, the stern-wheeler *Annabelle* hove into view from around an upstream bend and swung wide,

puffing black smoke, her paddle wheel slow-
ing, as she swung in toward the landing.

CHAPTER 2

"So you catch runaway niggers for a living?" "Chigger" Smealey said, eyeing his drinking companion in the smoky light of an overhead Rochester lamp. He was only into his second drink and still cautious around this stranger who'd bought the bottle they were sharing.

"Shh! Not so loud, Smealey," Gus Weir hissed, glancing around at the other men in the riverside tavern. "You want everybody in Keokuk to know my business?"

"I'd a thought most folks on the river would know you already if you been at this awhile," Smealey said.

"Hell, no!"

Smealey felt the obsidian eyes bore into him. He looked down and toyed with his glass. *This guy is fearsome; I'd best be careful.* Weir was a lean, muscular man, of about thirty-five — younger than Smealey. His collar-length black hair and black eyebrows

26

made his sun-bronzed skin even darker. The face was cloven by a straight nose that overhung a drooping black mustache, tinged with gray. Smealey had the uneasy feeling that looking dead-on into this man's face was like staring down a water moccasin.

"I operate in disguise, generally," Weir continued. "Sometimes I wear a wig, sometimes a beard, sometimes a fake scar or a putty nose. Use a bunch of aliases. That way if word slips out in some of these little burgs that a stranger's in the area, ain't nobody knows it's the same person who snagged a nigger offen a farm hereabouts only two weeks ago."

"Is Augustus Weir your real name?"

"Yeah. But it ain't Augustus. Gus is short for 'Gussage.' "

"What kinda name is that?" Smealey said before he thought.

But the hunter seemed to take no offense. "It means 'water gushing out of the ground.' Name of some place in the old country where my ancestors came from." He poured himself another drink. "What about you? Nobody's named 'Chigger.' "

"That's what I been called since I was knee-high to a katydid. My folks hung the name 'Chignall' on me — a village in England where my grandfather was born.

As a kid, I was little and wiry, and so m'friends slapped me with the nickname 'Chigger.' Better than 'Chignall' for sure. At least everybody knows what it means. Seems we're both named after some place across the ocean." Maybe he could strike some common ground with this man.

After a long minute of uneasy silence, Smealey thought maybe he'd said something to offend Weir, so he changed the subject. "So, how's the nigger-catching business?" He didn't care but felt he had to make conversation. As a straight-up robber and thief himself, he considered Weir's occupation akin to that of a bounty hunter — beneath his own dignity. But as long as the free drink was flowing, he wasn't about to say so.

"Well, business has slowed down considerable," Weir replied, topping off his shot glass. "These runaways are travelin' inland or farther north with the help of a few abolitionists. Not as many right along the river as used to be. Three, four years ago, I could take me a handful o' posters and cruise up and down along the Iowa and Illinois shore and snatch 'em offen these farms like scooping minnows in a seine. Same along the north bank of the Ohio. They run off from the plantations on the river down in Louisiana, mostly. And the rich planters there have the money to post substantial rewards. Some o' those healthy bucks cost upwards of three thousand dollars each at auction, so the owners can afford to pay me, or somebody, to bring 'em back in good shape."

"Not bein' nosey, but I reckon from what I seen o' those wanted posters, the reward money must be pretty good."

Weir nodded. "Yeah, there's money in it all right, but I have my travel expenses, too. This is a pretty chancy business and it ain't gonna last forever. That's why I'm doin' all I can to pile up a stash now."

"I reckon you run into lots o' trouble, too," Smealey said, sipping from his glass.

"That's for sure. I've had busted bones and been knocked over the head and shot at. See that there?" He pointed at a livid scar on his forearm that rested on the table. "Nigger knifed me. Fought like a wildcat, and I had to use a club on him. But I have to be careful. Can't damage the merchandise or it loses value."

The two men stopped talking as the burly bartender opened the nearby front door and blocked it with an empty keg. "Let some o' the smoke outa here," he said.

Smealey, accustomed to the miasma of the

29

place, barely noticed the difference, but did look out at the sweep of water below the bluff. Now, in the afterglow of sunset, the broad surface took on the hue of sliding quicksilver.

The two men continued to talk and drink as dusk deepened and the stars appeared over the tree line on the Illinois shore. After full dark the bartender returned and lighted the lantern that illuminated the swinging wooden sign over the door, announcing his establishment to the world as *The Oxblood*. It was Smealey's favorite hangout when he was in Keokuk.

When they were halfway through the second bottle, the worms were crawling in Smealey's brain, but he was still very much in control. His wariness had vanished, and he was toying with an idea that was, to him, nothing short of brilliant. In fact, he began to think that Fate had sent this man his way.

"So, where do you go from here?" Smealey asked. "You on the trail of somebody right now?"

"Naw. I wasted twelve days lookin' for one but found out he'd worked his way in amongst some free blacks as a deckhand on a steamer bound for Minnesota. The reward was only $200. Wasn't worth the time and effort to go that far. I'm on my way back to

New Orleans. I'll rest up a day or two and pick up a new batch o' wanted posters. There's others doin' this, too, but I work alone and have to stay ahead of the competition."

Smealey was silent for a few minutes, thinking, and stoking the fire with the fairly decent whiskey. The edge was off his sobriety now and the amber liquid trickled down his chin. He wiped it off with the back of his hand, feeling the rasping stubble of a four-day growth.

"As long as you're between jobs, I have a question for you," Smealey said after a bit.

"I'm listening."

"How do you feel about kidnapping?"

Weir glanced up sharply. "I'm a businessman. I ain't into that kinda stuff." There was no mistaking his grim refusal.

"Before you say 'No,' you might want to know there'd be at least $6,000 in gold for you."

Weir shook his head. "I know what you're gonna say, and the answer is still 'No.' I been asked to do this before when I fell on hard times. I ain't gonna snatch no free niggers and sell 'em back into slavery. I ain't good at forgin' papers on 'em so I can pull that off. And the penalty is too severe if you're caught."

31

"No, you got it all wrong. If I was talking about snatching free niggers there's a good one only a few miles from here working for a widow in St. Petersburg. He'd likely fetch top dollar, but he'd be a tough nut to crack. He ain't your average nigger." Smealey shook his head. "No. That ain't what I'm talkin' about at all. This has nothin' to do with niggers. Let me start at the beginning so you'll see the whole layout . . ." He leaned forward on his elbows so his voice would blend with the buzz of conversation in the dim room. "You ever hear of Injun Joe?"

"Sure, everybody has. That 'breed was a mean one, but he died in a cave down south of here a couple year ago. Wasn't he mixed up with a murder and some gold? I forget the details, but I read in the paper where two kids wound up with the gold."

"Right. Well, I was Injun Joe's pardner. That was *our* gold. Me and Joe found it hid in an old ramshackle house in the woods, likely buried by the Murrell gang a few years back. We took and hid it in that cave. Dumb luck those kids got mixed up in our business. Joe was locked in the cave by mistake and starved to death, and those two boys stumbled onto our stash and claimed it as

32

their own." Even retelling the tale made him angry.

Weir was staring at him with those hypnotic snake eyes.

Smealey dropped his gaze and continued, "Those two boys who wound up stealing *our* money — over $12,000 in gold coin, mind you — are named Tom Sawyer and Huckleberry Finn. They're both still living in St. Petersburg, struttin' around like gentry."

He paused to wet his whistle.

"Where's the gold now?" Weir asked, piercing eyes fixed on Smealey.

"A judge in that village name of Thatcher took charge of it for them. Don't know if it's in his safe or he invested it in their name 'cause those boys are underage." Smealey shrugged. "But he has access to it, even if it ain't right handy. Thatcher's a mighty important man in that town."

"Would these boys be a problem? They seem to have outsmarted you and Injun Joe."

Smealey felt a stab of anger at this jibe, but didn't show it. "One boy, Tom, lives with an aunt and the other, Huckleberry, is the son of the town drunkard. When his old man died, the kid was taken in by a rich widow."

"I see. But you feel sure they wouldn't be underfoot if you robbed the judge? We would want this to go smooth, without any rough stuff. The only law near that village is a few miles away at the county seat of Palmyra. I ain't above robbery if I'm forced to it by circumstances, mind you. But I prefer a legitimate occupation."

"This isn't about robbery, but I'll explain that in a minute. My pardner, Joe, is dead, so the gold is rightfully mine. But Fate took a hand and bad luck has done me out of my hard-won riches." He paused to sip. He had to slow down and stay in control. "It so happens this Judge Thatcher has a young daughter named Becky who's about thirteen or fourteen, and he thinks the world of her." Smealey was almost whispering now. "I'm sayin' we snatch the daughter, then send word to the judge she'll be returned safely if he forks over the $12,000 in gold. It's a very simple plan, and it don't involve violence or armed robbery. We can pull it off slicker 'an a hound's tooth."

"I don't know . . . High-toned, classy folks blow up like an overheated boiler when one of their own is taken for ransom — especially a kid."

"I'll go halves with you. How many niggers would you have to run down to earn that kind of cash?" He sat back, pleased with his cleverness. He emptied his glass, feeling the warm glow. "Once we have the gold and turn the girl loose unharmed, we split up and head for Texas or somers out west."

"Why don't you figure out a way to grab the whole $12,000 yourself?" Weir asked. "Why're you bringing me into this?"

"I never done anything like this before, and I need a man with your experience at snatching to make it work." Best to flatter Weir a little. "I figure that half o' that gold is better than none at all. And that's what I have now."

Weir studied his fingernails, then leaned back in his chair and crossed his legs.

Smealey had another part of his plan he'd hold in reserve for now to see if this man would take the offer. As hard-edged as Weir seemed, Smealey felt the slave-hunter was a man of his word. And he would know how to manage all the little details that needed to be thought of.

"When did you figure on doing this?"

"As soon as possible. Maybe tomorrow."

"Too soon. I need time to look over the village and the situation there with the girl and her father."

"How long would that take?"

"Hmmm . . . A day or two."

"Well, I was hanging around that village some last week. Saw one o' them society pieces in the newspaper that the judge was gonna send his daughter off to visit relatives in some little town down toward St. Louis for a few weeks soon as school let out for the summer."

Weir sat up straight. "What town? Is she traveling by herself? When is she leaving?" The rapid questions reminded Smealey of a hound catching a scent.

"Uh . . . Pretty sure it said this week, but can't recall if it gave the date."

"If you expect to carry this off, we must pay attention to the details. We'll take the steamboat down to St. Petersburg in the morning and nose around. If that girl is traveling alone, it should be a cinch to grab her — best if she goes by boat instead of coach."

"So you'll take the job?"

"We'll look over the layout. If I think there's a good chance it'll succeed, I'll take your offer for half the ransom."

"That's a relief," Smealey smiled and held out his hand.

Weir ignored it. "Go back to your place for a good night's sleep and I'll meet you at the riverfront in the morning at half past

36

nine. I was planning to take the *Annabelle* south anyway. I'll change my ticket to stop at St. Petersburg." He stood up from the table, but paused as Smealey took up the bottle by the neck. "Leave the rest o' that red-eye. No drinking until this is over. We both need to be sharp." He donned his broad-brimmed hat. "By the way, you won't recognize me; I'll be in disguise. I'll find *you.*" Then he melted through the open doorway and into the night.

CHAPTER 3

When Zane Rasmussen awoke, lying on his back, he instantly regretted having eaten that peanut bar covered with dark chocolate. His head was pounding, his stomach queasy.

The doctor had warned him. He should've listened. At age thirteen, he had enough sense to avoid eating things to which he was violently allergic without his mother having to hide them from him. But temptation proved too powerful and he'd given in.

He rationalized that he'd done it to gain weight for sports. Baseball wasn't a game that required a player to be heavy, but his teammates on the Rangers had begun calling him "stick man" and "slats" for his skinny arms and neck. He was strong enough to hit singles, and he was very quick. But the names were hurtful, nonetheless.

Zane lay still, eyes closed, trying to piece together shattered memory. He recalled sneaking down to the creek to eat the forbidden candy bar. That's where he'd had the severe reaction and vomited before everything went black. Maybe by regurgitating he'd rid himself of the peanuts and chocolate that poisoned his system. The doctor had said it wasn't uncommon for severe allergies to cause death.

He was terribly hot. Sweat poured off his face, trickling down his neck. Had he died and his soul been spirited away to Hell or Purgatory? Seized with sudden panic, he sprang to his feet. A wave of dizziness made him stagger. The glare off the white sand stabbed at his eyes. Could a dead person still feel dizzy or nauseated? No, no. The blood had rushed out of his head when he stood up too fast. If his blood was circulating, he had to be alive.

But where was he? Dreaming or in a coma? He didn't recognize anything around him. He took a few shuffling steps on the soft sandbar toward the nearby dark water. But this wasn't the creek where he often fished and had become sick. He raised his gaze. Not a creek at all; it was a broad river. The expanse of flowing water extended for at least a half-mile to the far shore.

Where was he, anyway? Along with feeling sick, he was now becoming seriously alarmed. He fumbled in his shirt pocket for his glasses, slipped them out of the case, and polished them on his shirttail.

The lenses brought the world into sharper focus. Maybe his blurred vision was contributing to his queasy stomach because as soon as he could see clearly, he began to feel a bit better.

He stood there uncertainly, not knowing what to do next. Then he recalled his cell phone clipped to his belt. He'd call his parents and ask them to come pick him up. But his hand hesitated on the phone. He didn't see any roads nearby. How could he tell them where he was? He didn't have a GPS. Oh well, he'd call anyway and tell them he'd passed out and now was lost. It would be good to hear a familiar voice.

The phone was still charged and he punched in his mother's cell number. If she wasn't available or didn't answer, he'd call his dad. One of them could come to his rescue. He'd have to admit to eating that nearly deadly candy bar, but he'd learned his lesson about that. If he wanted to gain weight and put on muscle it would be steak and potatoes and milkshakes from here on.

He held the phone to his ear. There was no sound of ringing on the other end. Dead silence. He ended the attempt, then tried again. Nothing. Then he punched in his father's number. Same result. He turned the phone off to save the battery.

A spasm of panic clenched his tender stomach. He swallowed. His mouth was dry and tasted terrible. Should he risk a drink of river water and possibly make himself even sicker? He slid the cell phone into its case on his belt and knelt by the river's edge. The water looked clear, but was no doubt swarming with microscopic organisms. He'd only rinse out his mouth. He slurped up a handful, swirled it around his tongue, and spat, then repeated the process. It was warm and tasted like fish and dirt. The new foul taste replaced the old foul taste. He stuck out his tongue and wiped it with his sleeve, but forgot his shirt was covered with sand. Ugh! He pulled out his handkerchief and cleaned the inside of his mouth as best he could of the grit and taste. At least the folded handkerchief was clean. But with all the sweating and loss of his stomach contents, he was dehydrated and very thirsty. If he tried to drink this river water, there was a good chance he'd be sick again.

He had to find a road and flag down a car and ask for help. But, looking around for some shade, he noticed for the first time he

41

was standing on a long sandbar at the upstream end of an island, and the chute between the narrow island and the eastern shore was only about forty yards wide. Was there a bridge to the other side of this river?

Drifting downstream near the far shore was what looked like a flatboat with a man at the long steering oar. There was no sound of a diesel or gasoline engine.

He'd satisfied himself he wasn't dead, but this had to be a dream. With the coming of spring, he'd re-read both the novels about Tom Sawyer and Huckleberry Finn, as well as perusing two or three books written by his grandfather who was a Mark Twain scholar. So he had all these adventures of the 1840s fresh on his mind — and now they were replaying themselves, surfacing from his subconscious in a dream. This thought calmed his fears for now. He was sometimes conscious in a dream of the fact that he *was* dreaming. And that was the case now.

Zane dreamed vividly and often, usually in color. His nocturnal visions were rarely fearful nightmares, but were always adventurous or exciting about things he'd been doing — travel, watching TV or playing video games, sports, and — like now — being lost somewhere and trying to find his way home. When comparing notes with his classmates and friends about this, he discovered they also dreamed. It was a common enough experience, but they denied having as many or as exciting dreams as he did. He attributed it to an active imagination.

What to do next? He walked toward the deep woods, about thirty yards away, to seek relief from the hot sun. Hundred-foot trees and green undergrowth covered what he could see of the island to the south.

It felt at least ten degrees cooler in the shade, and he reveled in the slight breeze — until the mosquitoes began to buzz around his ears and sweaty face.

He was in the act of swatting them when he looked up and saw a rowboat containing three people approaching the sandbar. Good. He could find out where he was and call for help.

Stepping out of the woods, he walked toward the approaching boat.

His stomach had settled down and, except for his thirst, he felt better.

The boy who was rowing paused to look over his shoulder when the black man at the tiller pointed toward shore.

Zane didn't care who these people were; they represented help and possibly a way home. They must be poor fishermen, he

43

thought, or they'd have an outboard motor. He couldn't remember the last time he'd seen anyone using oars.

The prow grounded on the sand and the three piled out and pulled the boat up higher.

"Hi!"

"Hullo, yourself," the slightly shorter boy with light-brown hair greeted him. "Who're you?"

"Zane Rasmussen." He offered his hand and they shook.

"I'm Tom Sawyer, and this here's Huckleberry Finn."

They gripped hands.

"And this is our friend, Jim." The black man hesitated, then took the proffered hand.

Tom and Huck and Jim? Who'd they think they were kidding? Maybe they think I haven't read the books.

"Nice to know ya," Zane said.

"You from around here?" Tom asked, eyeing him suspiciously. "You look like you might be part Injun."

"I'm American — like you. My mother is of Chinese descent."

"What're you doing here?"

"I'm lost."

"Where's your boat?" Tom was leading the way toward the shelter of trees.

44

"Uh . . . I don't have one."

"You swum over?" He glanced at Zane's plaid shirt and khaki pants. His gaze lingered on the white tennis shoes.

"No." Might as well tell the truth no matter how strange it sounded. "I got sick and passed out. Woke up here."

"Maybe you fell in the river upstream and drifted down to this sandbar. Or maybe somebody threw you off a steamboat," Tom surmised. "But you been here a while 'cause your clothes dried out."

"If you's out cold and fell in dis river, you likely drown," Jim said, " 'less you's floatin' on yo back."

They seemed genuinely concerned about trying to figure out this mystery.

"Where am I?" Zane asked.

"That's St. Petersburg over yonder." Tom jabbed a thumb over his shoulder.

"What state?"

"You *are* mighty confused. Missouri, of course."

"What? I passed out in Delaware."

"Where's that?" Huck asked.

"Don't you recollect your history?" Tom was scornful. "One of the colonies. And it's a blamed long way from here. Off east somers."

45

"You sho you wasn't hit on de head?" Jim asked.

Zane wasn't sure of anything now. His first instinct was to suspect his friends of an elaborate practical joke. Maybe one of them would pop out from behind a tree any second. His next thought, more fearful, was that he'd lost his sanity. Perhaps he'd eaten some bad mushrooms on that pizza he'd had after his baseball game. That, along with the allergic reaction to the candy bar he'd scarfed up later, might be causing hallucinations. He took a deep breath to calm himself and wiped a sleeve across his sweaty face.

"I was reading about you three," he said, deciding to play along for now.

"About us?" Huck asked.

"Sure. You're all characters in a book."

"Well, don't that beat all?" Tom grinned. "We're even more famous than I thought. What book? Who wrote it?"

Zane knew he was being had, but would continue with this Alice-in-Wonderland scenario to see where it led. "There are two books — *The Adventures of Tom Sawyer* and *Adventures of Huckleberry Finn.* Written by Mark Twain."

"Mark who?" Tom asked. "Never heard of him. How does he know us?"

"Okay, enough is enough. I like a joke as

good as anyone, but, seriously, I need your help to find my way home." Zane was now convinced he was dreaming. And dreams generally didn't make much sense.

Jim was staring, wide-eyed, at him. "Witches likely fetched you here. Lots of 'em be flyin' 'roun in de dark o' de moon."

Zane ignored the comment. "I tried calling my parents, but my phone won't work." He withdrew his cell phone from its case, and held it up.

"You're talkin' outa your head," Tom said, taking the instrument and turning it over in his hands. "What *is* this thing?"

"Unless you been on Jupiter for the last forty years, you'd know what that is — a cell phone. And there are models a lot newer and fancier than that one."

"I think you're the one who's been on Jupiter — or maybe just now come from there."

Zane saw they were talking at cross-purposes. He began to feel uneasy. If he were not dreaming, he had in reality traveled from another time as well as another place. "Look," he began, "I need to find a way home. I have a little money. If you guys could take me over to that little town maybe I can catch a Greyhound back to Delaware."

"Here, sit down and lean back against this

47

tree," Tom said. "I think maybe you been out in the hot sun too long."

Zane did as directed. "You boys have anything to drink? I'm dyin' of thirst." His tongue felt as if it were coated with half-dried glue. "I guess it'd be too much to ask if you had a cold Coke or a Dr Pepper?"

"What's that?"

"Thought so. Any kind of soda will do."

"My Aunt Polly drinks soda water when her stomach's upset," Tom said.

"No, no. Not bicarb. This would be like . . ." he tried to think of some long-gone soft drink he'd read about. "Sarsaparilla."

"All we have is a canteen of water in the boat," Huck said. "I'll fetch it."

Zane was beginning to feel dizzy and hoped he wasn't about to throw up again. He leaned his head back against the rough bark of the giant oak.

"When we was over here playin' pirates a couple years ago, we found a spring on this island," Tom said. "Not sure I could find it again, if it's still here after the floods."

A minute later Huck returned and handed him a blanket-sided two-quart canteen. Zane chugged down several swallows of the lukewarm water. He stopped to take a breath, then had another drink. "Thanks."

He handed back the canteen. "Wonder how much a bus ticket is?" He dug into his side pocket and pulled out some change — several pennies, a nickel, two dimes, and a quarter. "Wait." He withdrew a wallet from a hip pocket and extracted two ones and a five. "That's not enough to ride the Greyhound from Missouri to Delaware," he groaned. For the time being, he had to assume all this was real. He was stuck here, unless he could make his cell phone work.

"Lemme see that." Tom held out his hand.

Zane handed over his money.

Tom held up a penny between thumb and forefinger. "This says, *One Cent.* Money must be cheap where you come from. Here's a *real* penny." He dug into his pocket and produced a large copper coin about the size of a quarter, but thicker.

Zane looked at it — the head of Lady Liberty and the date of 1849.

"And I never seen bank notes like this around here," Tom continued. "Maybe they was issued by a St. Louis bank."

"You know right well the federal treasury printed those," Zane said. He was tiring of this joke.

Huck was turning over the coins. "Tom, these here sure look real, but they must be from some other country." He looked at them carefully in the sunlight. "No . . . it says right here, 'United States of America.' "

Tom examined the quarter. "And this one has a picture of George Washington on it."

They all looked at each other with blank expressions.

In spite of the heat, a chill went over Zane.

"Appears to me what we have here," Tom said slowly as if revealing a great truth, "is a boy from some other time — likely the future. Just you take a look at all the evidence," he said, assuming the role of detective. "He don't know how he come to be here. He's talkin' about ridin' a greyhound, which everybody knows is a skinny, fast dog; he's wearin' shoes in the summertime and they're made out of some kind of canvas and not leather; he's usin' spectacles which ain't worn by nobody but old people." He took hold of the cuff of Zane's shirt between thumb and forefinger. "This here shirt's been sewed by a machine in a factory somers; he's carrying strange money that he says is made by the United States government; he says he can talk to his parents through that little box on his belt. He asks for a strange drink that some doctor has put pepper in. He is part Chinese. Now, I ask you, if that ain't proof he's from another time, then this ain't 1849."

50

Zane's stomach contracted. "Oh my God! Is this really 1849? Then I've somehow traveled back almost two hundred years into the past." He was feeling an empty panic as if he were leaning too far over the edge of a cliff.

"Don't worry about it," Tom said, still acting as spokesman for the other two. "I'm acceptin' of it, if you are. Lots of strange things in this world we can't understand — like steam locomotives and balloons that fly over the ocean, and the workings of Providence. But while you're here, we can have lots of fun. Then we'll see about starting you back to your home." He turned to Zane who was still sitting with his back to the tree. "We was discussin' plans to go adventurin' over in the territory, and you can come with us."

"No . . . I need to be on my way. My folks . . ."

"Your folks, my granny!" Tom said. "They ain't nowhere's close to even bein' born yet."

CHAPTER 4

All four of them eventually agreed, for lack of a better explanation, that Zane had come here from another time and place.

Because this newcomer was human, like them, Tom declared that Zane was not from another planet.

For a half hour or more they discussed the "how" and "why" of it with various degrees of insight and many unanswered questions.

"Should we ask Judge Thatcher or Widow Douglas or even the schoolmaster, Mister Dobbins, if they can explain this?" Tom wondered.

"What about the preacher?" Huck asked. "He knows all about angels and ghostly stuff."

Zane shook his head. "You can bet these grown-ups don't have any better ideas about traveling through time than anyone else," he said. "I think it's contrary to most religious beliefs. As a matter of fact, they'd think you — we — were all crazy or had sunstroke or something."

"But they've all lived longer and maybe come across this before, even if they don't know what causes it," Tom said.

"More 'an likely a steamboat pilot or cap'n woulda knowed some travelers through time," Huck opined. "They prob'ly met thousands of folks on the river — more 'an the preacher or the schoolmaster."

"Dey could 'splain it if dey believed in witches," Jim said.

"Yeah, but none of those folks believe in witches," Tom said. "So we'd best keep mum about this for now, 'cause we ain't able to show 'em no proof that it's real."

Zane pushed back his shirtsleeve and looked at his watch. "Hey, guys, I feel okay now. It's past one o'clock and I'm hungry."

"What's that on your arm?"

"My watch."

"Never saw a watch that little," Tom said. "That's right handy."

"The widow, she wears a little gold watch on a chain around her neck," Huck said. "And she can pin it on her shirtwaist, too."

Zane took it off and let Huck and Tom examine this curiosity. "It's all sweaty and dirty now. Sunlight keeps it running."

"What?"

"Yeah. Like sun keeps plants growing."

"Another of the wonders from your time, I reckon," Tom said, handing it back.

"You ever see one of these?" Zane continued, slipping a rollerball pen from his shirt pocket. He clicked it open and wrote a few squiggles on a computer receipt from Benito's Pizza Parlor. Both proved to be items of wonderment.

Zane explained them, then decided to have even more fun. "Here's something I bet you haven't seen." He pulled aside the fly flap on his khakis and worked the zipper up and down. "It's called a zipper."

"If dat don't beat all," Jim marveled. "No buttons or ties to keep de britches shut."

"Another wonder of the twenty-first century," Zane said. "But I read where it was invented a hundred years before these pants were made. Elias Howe, who also invented the sewing machine, patented something like it in 1851 but didn't do anything with it. A handy little mechanism."

"Guess you call it a zipper 'cause o' the noise it makes," Tom said. "Wish that'd been my invention. I woulda slapped a patent on it and had a bunch of factories boomin' like thunder, and scads o'money a'rollin in."

"You's already rich, Mars Tom," Jim reminded him.

"That's right. We do have plenty o' money," Tom nodded at Huck. "Coming over the river, you said you was dead set against lighting out for the territory with us for a few weeks of wild adventures amongst the Injuns. What if I told you me and Huck was discussin' helpin' you buy your family out of bondage if you come along with us?"

Jim opened and closed his mouth a time or two like a fish out of water. Then tears began to well up in the man's dark eyes. He blinked them away and looked down. "Dat's mighty kind of you, Mars Tom, and you too, Huck. But I can't take yo money. I gots to do dis myself. I gots to take care of my own."

Zane started to speak up and tell them they could save their money, that everything would work out for the best because Lincoln would free the slaves. But then he realized the Thirteenth Amendment ending slavery was still sixteen years in the future. Anything might happen between now and then. They couldn't wait. So Zane swallowed back this piece of information. He marveled that he was beginning to feel like he was part of a nineteenth-century world.

They talked on for a time and swore they would keep mum about this traveler from another time.

"But you and Jim need to say if you wanta go over to the territory with me and Huck," Tom said.

Zane and Jim looked at each other.

"I don't have any choice," Zane said with a shrug. "As long as I'm here I need somebody to look out for me. If I'm left on my own and start talking and acting like an alien, the law will throw me in jail or a mental hospital or insane asylum." He nodded. "Yeah, sign me up for the trip. I'm sure it beats summer camp in New Jersey."

"What about you, Jim?" Tom asked. "Can't nothin' convince you to come along? It'd be just like old times. We need a grown man to rely on — in case o' trouble."

Jim was silent for a few moments. "I do wants to go, but mebbe I be temptin' de Almighty by taking mo' chances. Providence done delivered me from some mighty scary 'ventures awready. And I needs to be workin' and earnin' my pay . . ."

"Tell you what, Jim," Tom interjected, "since you won't let us buy your family, me and Huck'll furnish your outfit and pay you double what you'd make in wages while you're away, to make up for the dangersome part of the trip."

"Dat's mighty considerate, Mars Tom."

He removed his floppy hat and ran a callused hand over his curly mat. "If dat be de way of it, I reckon I'll go. The widow, she just have to do widout me, like she done befoe."

"Then it's all settled," Tom said.

"As a stranger here, I'll need some coaching," Zane remarked.

"I think while we're collectin' our traps, you'd best stay here on the island," Tom said. "We'll bring over food and water — and an old blanket to keep off the damps at night. It'll take a day or so to pry enough money outa the judge and to buy our outfits. I hope you can ride a horse."

Zane had never been on a horse, but this wasn't the time to say so.

"What about Aunt Polly and the widow?" Huck asked.

"I'll have to think on that," Tom said. "We'll come up with a good story for them, or else we can sneak off in the night and leave 'em a note."

"I hates to do dat, Mars Tom. De widow, she been mighty square wid me," Jim said.

"Yeah, me, too," Huck added. "And the widow can spot a lie faster 'an she can spot a gravy stain on a white tablecloth."

"Hmm . . . Lemme think on it awhile," Tom said. "I'll come up with a plan."

The four of them shuffled through the sand to the boat.

"Here's the canteen," Tom said, tossing it to Zane. "We'll row back over this evenin' and fetch food and a blanket. We'll catch some catfish for supper, build a fire, fry 'em up, and have a high old time. Maybe I can even lift a jug o' cider from Auntie's root cellar." He pushed the skiff back off the sandbar and stepped in. "I'll find you a straw hat and some old clothes so you won't look like you're from Jubiter." He took his place with the oars as the current began to drift the boat.

Gripping the canteen, Zane watched them go. He felt more relaxed now that he had a few friends in this alien world. But at the same time, part of his brain was thinking there was a good chance he'd wake up from this dream very soon. If he did, he wouldn't have to explain baseball or bicycles or computers to them.

CHAPTER 5

Zane stared after the receding boat — he'd have to become accustomed to calling it a "skiff." Apparently, there were different kinds of rowing boats of which he had no knowledge. He admired the deft way Tom handled his oars, angling the vessel upstream and across the pull of the current.

When the boat was halfway to the far shore, Zane shouldered the canteen strap and started toward the woods. For now, he'd have to be the stranger here and try to learn the details of living in this world. Current time here had seemed like only vague, historic time before.

He broke off a stick the size of a small baseball bat from a driftwood log half buried in the sand. It was good to have a weapon against snakes while he spent the afternoon exploring.

The vegetation under the canopy of trees was surprisingly sparse, due to lack of

59

sunlight and periodic flooding that scoured the island. A hundred paces into the green twilight, he discovered a shallow pool ten yards long and about five wide. The muddy margin of the pool was crisscrossed with delicate prints of deer hooves.

He continued on, seeing no sign of snakes, but avoiding wading through deep grass or weeds where he couldn't see his feet. In his world he'd not spent as much time in the woods as he had on the soccer or baseball fields, or playing video games. He was sure the boys here spent most of their waking hours outdoors in good weather, inventing their own games, since there were no team sports organized by adults. And the absence of air-conditioning would have kept them outside all summer anyway.

He continued south along the narrow island, swinging the stick, enjoying the smell of late-blooming honeysuckle vines. Now and then he paused to inhale their fragrance, disturbing honey bees at work. Were all bees attracted to sweet-smelling flowers *and* rotten-smelling ones? Or, were different kinds of bees drawn to each? Did the type of flower affect the way the honey tasted? He gazed off toward the wooded bluffs on the Missouri shore, thinking how little he knew of the natural world.

After a mile or more, he was in the thickest part of the woods in a pale-green twilight. The afternoon sun penetrated through the heavy overhead canopy only in the shifting, scattered freckles of light on the forest floor. He was amazed at the silence. No roaring motorcycles or diesel trucks, no jet planes, no ripping lawn mowers or weed eaters, no wailing sirens or blaring horns, no rock bands with earth-shattering amps. The sighing of the wind in the boughs far overhead reached his ears as a soothing hum, softer than an electric fan.

Had there ever been a documented case of time travel before now? He recalled a recent TV show that explored mysterious disappearances in the Bermuda triangle. The pilot of a small plane had been interviewed. He stated that when flying west across the Caribbean, he'd experienced a sensation of entering a long tunnel in the clouds. His clock had malfunctioned. When he came out of the cloud again and made contact with a Florida control tower to find his position, he discovered he'd traveled at least 400 miles in only a few minutes, even though the maximum speed of his small plane was a shade over 150 miles per hour. Time and distance had somehow been compressed. Time apparently was not an absolute, immovable barrier.

Zane shook his head to clear the mental gyrations of trying to imagine such a thing.

The swinging canteen brushed against his leg and he felt a lump in the side pocket of his pants. A pack of sunflower seeds! He'd forgotten he had them. A good snack to stave off hunger for several hours until supper. He poured out a small handful and popped them into his mouth. Holding them in one cheek, he cracked and ate the seeds, spitting shells as he walked along.

Directly he came abreast of a narrow, rocky ridge on his left, layers of gray limestone covered in vines and small bushes growing out of the crevices. A good place for rattlesnakes, he thought, and gave it wide berth as he continued on.

He eventually reached the foot of the island, nearly three miles from where he'd started, and came out of the forest to a muddy shore that dropped off into the dark current swirling past. Glancing at his watch, he saw that it was nearly three o'clock. By the time he reached the upstream sandbar again his new friends might be returning.

As he turned to re-enter the woods, he heard a strange coughing noise and looked out to see a stern-wheel steamboat toward the far shore churning upstream out of the main channel. No pounding diesel towboats here; no strings of steel barges.

He plunged into the woods again, heading back. He felt himself becoming more and more relaxed. There was no ball practice, no school or exams to worry about, no allergist appointments, no TV shows to watch, no urgent meetings that required his parents to drive him here and there, no way to email or text his friends. His former hectic schedule did not exist. And so far, he'd had no time to become bored. He hadn't even thought about his non-working cell phone in more than two hours. He thought of his little sister, Miranda, who was three years younger. Was she wondering where he was? If Tom Sawyer was right, she hadn't been born yet. Neither had he, come to think of it.

He'd timed his hike exactly. When he again emerged on the open sandbar at the head of the island, he saw a skiff approaching from upstream and it was late afternoon.

His new friends debarked with a sack of food, a jug of cider and one of buttermilk, fishing lines, a skillet, tin plates and cups, and a striped blanket. They dumped it all on the hard sand near the tree line.

In no time, Jim started a driftwood fire and Tom was laying out the plates with cornbread and turnip greens on the blanket, while Huck was setting some lines for fish.

"We told Aunt Polly and the widow we was camping out over here tonight," Tom said, slicing some bacon with his Barlow knife. "They was agreeable."

"They don't worry about you drowning in this river without life jackets, or anything?" Zane said — then wished he'd kept quiet. It made him sound like a sissy.

"Naw. After what we been through, they figure we can take care of ourselves without no help," Tom grinned. "We give 'em plenty to worry about these past two years, so our campin' here sure ain't gonna bother 'em none. We're prob'ly safe as if we was sleepin' in our own beds."

"What's a life jacket?" Huck asked, expertly skinning a small mudcat he'd taken off his line a few minutes before.

"It's like a regular vest, except that it has cork sewn into it so it floats and holds you up if you can't swim or are hurt or something." No sense trying to explain foam flotation. He'd have to quit using terms they didn't understand. "In most states it's a law you have to wear them in small boats."

"Why do folks who make de laws care if you drowns?" Jim asked.

"I don't know. Guess it causes a lot of

trouble to haul your body out of the river. I suppose it pollutes the water." Zane made up his mind to give whatever answer seemed plausible without trying to analyze these questions. "Speaking of pollution, do you think that catfish is safe to eat?" he asked, thinking of the mercury its flesh might have absorbed.

"Ain't no reason it shouldn't be safe," Tom said, eyeing him as if he were paranoid. "Why? You reckon it's gonna poison you or sumpthin'? Nothin' better'an fresh fried catfish — if you don't drink sweet milk with it. You have to drink the buttermilk we fetched over."

"I . . . uh . . . I'm sure it's fine." This was 1849. No need to eat only farm-raised grain-fed catfish. There were no chemical pesticides sprayed from crop-dusting planes to be washed into the river from adjoining farmlands. His father had told him he'd been on the river and seen it covered for a quarter-mile with a layer of what looked like soap suds more than two feet thick.

Tom dished up some limp turnip greens, which Zane didn't recall eating before. "Now, poke salet," Tom continued, "that's a whole different kettle o' fish."

"Das right," Jim added. "If you picks a mess o' dem greens, you'd best boil 'em up right smart."

"If you don't," Tom said, "poke salet'll do more than tickle your gizzard — it'll knock a body stiff and cold as river ice. But Aunt Polly, she don't fix that no more since we have plenty other stuff to eat."

Talk of food poisoning was just the thing he needed to stimulate his appetite, Zane thought, ruefully — at a time when he was trying to gain weight.

The sun had slid below the bluffs when they finished their meal. It was nearing the longest day of the year when twilight seemed to stretch out long past bedtime.

Zane had eaten two helpings of everything and was feeling much better. "Wow! That was good. I was empty." Content, he sipped the tangy cider from a tin cup. He leaned back on his elbow, eyeing the dying fire. The sparse meal was even better than the picnic his family had hosted at his last birthday with homemade potato salad, barbecue, and baked beans. It would take time for him to quit comparing everything in this new world to things in his old.

Huck and Jim pulled out their pipes and lit up. But Tom abstained. No one asked Zane if he wanted to smoke.

"Wish I had my harmonica," Zane said.

"What's that?" Tom asked.

I've done it again, Zane thought. "It's . . . uh . . . sometimes called a mouth harp."

"Like a Jew's harp?"

"No, nothing like that. It's a little metal instrument with holes in it. You blow into it and suck on it to make different notes. Very smooth music — kind of like a little pipe organ. I think it was invented in Germany at some time or other." He didn't want to go into the fact that it came to the states decades after 1849. He found himself wishing he had paid more attention to his classes in American history.

They chatted until dusk began to sidle up from the west, drawing its gray mantle silently over the island and the small party around the glowing coals. Jim added two small logs to the fire to forestall the mosquitoes and mayflies. But it was still so warm they had to sit well back from the blaze for comfort.

No one brought up the topic of traveling back from the future or it's unsolvable mysteries. Instead, Tom was all for talking up their forthcoming adventures in the territory. Huck and Jim caught some of his enthusiasm when he described from his imagination the tribes of Indians they'd meet, the gold-seekers they'd pass on the trail, the meals of roasted buffalo hump

67

dripping succulent juices into the fire.

Zane listened mostly in silence. He'd seen western movies and documentaries of the plains and western states, and had his own ideas of what they would look like. It was difficult to picture the wide-open spaces as they would be now without highways, small towns, and gas stations. He'd never been there, but had flown over the plains at 30,000 feet on his way to visit relatives in California. However, now was not the time to bring up *that* subject.

"Reckon those clothes will fit ya?" Tom asked during a lull in the conversation, indicating the pants and shirt he'd tossed onto the blanket.

Zane stood up and shucked off his trousers and pulled on the ones Tom had brought. The brown canvas pants were of a heavy material, and a bit short, but they would suffice. They had only one suspender and no belt loops. The four pockets would hold his billfold, cell phone, handkerchief, change, and comb. The shirt, with widely spaced vertical red stripes, had no collar, and fuller sleeves than he was used to, but it was a decent fit and felt good against his skin.

"Yeah, this is fine," he said.

"Unless you go barefoot like us, I reckon

you'll have to wear those white shoes," Tom said. "Maybe we can dirty 'em up some so nobody'll notice."

Zane looked down at his low-cut sneakers. They were almost new and felt good on his feet with the padded sweat socks. "I'm not used to running around barefoot," he said. "Too much chance of cutting my feet on sharp rocks or broken glass. Besides, I could pick up hookworms . . ." He paused and saw Tom and Huck look at each other and shake their heads. He'd have to quit saying things like that. "I'll wear my own shoes," he stated. He reached for the straw hat with the ragged brim on one side. It fit well enough.

"De sun be mighty fearsome 'round dees parts in de summertime," Jim said. "You needs dat hat."

"Yeah. And now you can pass for a boy who lives along the river," Tom said. "I reckon we can say you're up from a village near St. Louis or somers, visiting kin over in Palmyra for the summer."

Zane slid his belt out of his old pants and buckled it around his new pants. "In case this suspender breaks," he explained. He was so lean he often couldn't keep his pants up unless his belt was snugged up to the last notch. Tomorrow he'd use his knife to punch three or four slits in the pants around the waist to thread the belt through.

The night wore on and directly the conversation lagged. The fire burned down and the small logs fell in on themselves, leaving only glowing red coals. The starlit blackness arched over them, and one by one each stretched out to sleep.

Long after the other three were snoring, Zane lay awake, his old fears and uncertainties returning. His mind played out in detail all the events of the day. A cool dampness crept up from the river. He listened for sounds of the night. Crickets chirping. Bullfrogs croaking in the shallows. Occasionally a fish splashed somewhere. But he didn't hear the heavy splashing caused by Asian carp that had invaded the river in his own time. A few lightning bugs blinked silently on and off. For now, there was nothing he could do about where he was or what was happening. As Shakespeare or somebody once said, "Time was out of joint." He would work toward figuring out a way home. Then he thought, *If I go to sleep I'll wake up in my own bed and realize this was only a dream.*

He relaxed and slowly drifted off.

CHAPTER 6

The sound of someone yelling stirred Zane from deep sleep. He rose slowly from a half-formed dream. For a few seconds, he didn't know where he was. Hadn't summer vacation started? Why did he have to get out of bed so early?

"Jim! Huck! Wake up. Look!"

Tom Sawyer's voice. Zane rolled over and cracked his eyelids. He was lying partly on sand, partly on a blanket. He wasn't at home. So it hadn't been a dream after all.

The strident clanging of a distant brass bell shattered the early morning stillness.

"What be all de blim-blammin'?" Jim complained.

Zane pushed himself to a sitting position and reached for his sneakers.

Huck was digging the sleep out of one eye with a fist as he struggled to his feet.

Tom stood at the edge of the bar several yards away, pointing toward the village. The

71

sun had not yet cleared the trees on the Illinois side. Wisps of gray mist rose from the river, while the village still lay in shadow.

"They don't ring that ferry bell like that 'less sumpin' mighty important is happenin'," Tom declared.

Hardly were the words out of his mouth when a column of white spurted from the top of a packet boat at the landing. A second or two later, the deep bellow of a steam whistle reached their ears.

They gathered at the water's edge and strained to see what was happening in the village.

It was too distant and too dark for Zane to make out anything much except the gray outlines of several white buildings.

"We best be gittin' over there," Huck said. "Last time folks was so riled up was when you and Becky slithered outa that cave like you was risin' from the dead."

"I hope they's celebratin' good news o' some kind." Tom was already scrambling to collect their utensils and throw them into a cloth sack.

Jim was shaking out their blankets and Huck went to kick sand on the remains of the campfire.

Zane took his pocketknife, jabbed several slits in the waist of his pants, then threaded his belt through the holes and buckled it. Before he clipped the small leather case to his belt, he took a quick look at his cell phone. It lit up with four bars so it was still charged, but he didn't waste time trying to use it. He rolled up the clothes he'd been wearing when he arrived and stuffed them into one of the canvas sacks.

The four of them hauled their gear to the nearby skiff and dumped it in, then climbed in after it.

"Gimme de oars," Jim said.

There was no argument. Jim took up his position on the middle thwart and Huck and Tom pushed off. Zane scrambled in and tried to stay out of the way.

The boat swung out into the current, and Jim laid to his work, digging deep and stroking long. Tom sat at the tiller, but there was no need to steer. Aimed high, the prow of the skiff cut the water as if the current wasn't even there. Jim's powerful shoulder muscles bunched under his shirt and he rotated the oars in a practiced rhythm, thrusting the boat ahead like it was being propelled by a small outboard motor.

After a time, they rowed upstream of the town and Jim lay on his oars to drift. Then, with a few well-timed strokes, he brought the boat in and grounded it on the cobblestones at the upper end of the landing.

As they jumped out, Huck whispered, "Where'd you borrow this boat? Best not be leavin' it here."

"Never mind," Tom said. "Nobody's gonna notice. I'll move it later."

The ferryman had stopped ringing the brass bell when they were halfway over the river, much to the relief of Zane's ears.

They ran up toward Main Street, which paralleled the river — all but Jim who was ambling along slowly behind, apparently still winded. Even though Jim was free, it struck Zane that perhaps this kindly black man had become accustomed to not walking along with whites in public. Zane was rapidly becoming familiar with the standing of blacks in this earlier world.

The sun's early rays were beginning to lance down, lighting the tops of the whitewashed buildings. Full daylight had come.

People hurried past on the boardwalk; others were standing in groups of two or three talking urgently among themselves. The tension along the street reminded Zane of a humming, vibrating cable on a high-voltage steel tower.

Tom grabbed a small boy starting into the newspaper office.

"Hey, what's all the ruckus?"

"Where you been?" the boy asked in a high-pitched voice. "You know Judge Thatcher? His girl's been kidnapped."

"What?"

"Yeah. Becky." He jerked his arm free. "Lemme go. Special edition is out."

Tom leaned against the wall, staring straight ahead, a stunned look on his face.

"Tom!" Huck shook him by the shoulder, but Tom only wobbled and slumped to a sitting position in the doorway.

Zane and Huck locked glances. "We have to do something," Zane said.

About that time Jim caught up with them. He took one look at Tom's vacant, pale face. "Is you ailin', chile? You looks powerful sick — like a mule hauled off and kicked you in a hurtsome place."

"Becky Thatcher's been kidnapped," Zane told him.

"Oh, Lawdy!" Jim took a step backward.

Before anyone could speak again, a young man in a white shirt jogged across the street toward them.

"You, Tom! Tom Sawyer!" He stopped, out of breath, hands on his knees. "Judge Thatcher wants to see you and Huckleberry at his house right away," he gasped. "It's urgent." He looked from one to the other of the boys. "I'm his law clerk," he panted when nobody moved or answered. "The judge sent me to find you two. I been lookin' all over town when your aunt said you weren't home. Follow me."

Huck took Tom by the arm and pulled him erect. Tom's knees buckled and he nearly fell until Jim grabbed him under the other arm.

"This way." The clerk started off at a brisk walk with Tom being half-dragged along behind. Zane followed in their wake.

Much of the residential area of St. Petersburg was built on a steep slope that pitched up away from the downtown area along the river.

Zane slogged along, leaning into the hill and puffing after three blocks of steady climbing, his thighs begging for mercy. Worse than soccer practice, he thought.

By the time they reached the two-story frame house, Tom had his feet under him after a fashion, but still hadn't spoken a word.

The clerk led them through the front door into a spacious parlor and then through an arched doorway on the left into the dining room. The room held the delicious aroma of fried sausage. A scattering of breakfast things covered one end of the long table.

"Here they are, Judge." The clerk silently

slid away and let himself out the front door.

"Tom and Huck! Thank God you're here." Judge Thatcher came forward with outstretched hands. "Sit down. Sit down."

Tom fell into a captain's chair near the head of the table, and Huck, Zane, and Jim sat on the straight chairs.

The judge was upwards of forty or so, Zane thought, well fleshed, in a collarless white shirt and unshaven.

The judge raked his fingers through dark auburn hair, and stared at them through puffy eyes. "You boys hungry?" Without waiting for an answer, he turned to a middle-aged black woman in the doorway. "Elsa hustle up some more pancakes and coffee for us, please."

Was this woman a paid cook or a slave?

A slight movement caught Zane's eye and for the first time he noticed another man in the room. Leaning against the mantel with an unlit cigar in his mouth was a tall, white-haired gent with a drooping mustache. A badge was pinned to his vest.

"I guess you've heard the terrible news by now," the judge said. He walked up and down, wringing his hands. "Becky has been taken." The judge appeared ready to break out in tears. His lips trembled and he turned away toward the wall. A second later, he faced about and sat down heavily on one of the padded dining chairs. He took a deep, shuddering breath and was silent for a few moments.

The four who had come from the island looked at each other. Zane felt very sorry for this man's pain.

When no one spoke, the tall man came forward, taking the cigar from his mouth, and put a reassuring hand on the judge's shoulder. He cleared his throat. "I'm Sheriff Reuben Stiles from the county seat at Palmyra. I heard the news three hours ago when the judge's clerk rode over and roused me out of bed." He pulled out a chair and seated himself. "Now that you boys are here, we can discuss this matter logically and see what can be done."

The judge, apparently needing something physical to steady his trembling hands, rose to pour coffee for everyone. By the time he finished, the cook came back in with a tray of steaming pancakes, a pitcher of syrup, and a huge blob of butter.

The judge sure knew how to live, Zane thought, pouring thick cream into his coffee from a silver pitcher. The glassware was white china with delicate flowered borders.

"Judge, tell me again exactly what happened," Sheriff Stiles said. "Take your time and give all the details you can remember."

The judge paused a moment, appearing to collect his thoughts. "I was taking Becky down to Marsville to visit her cousins for the rest of June. My late wife's sister and her husband have three children and the family lives on eighty acres of good bottomland outside that village. It's about twenty-five miles south of here. I hired a one-horse rig — a light buggy — from Charley Bowden over at the livery," he continued. "I was planning to spend a day or two there myself and then return." He paused to take a sip of coffee. His hands were now steady, Zane noted.

"Becky packed her things in a leather grip and we started just after sunup yesterday so we could arrive before dark. After all the floods this spring, there are still parts of the river road that are washed out, and I knew we'd likely have to make a few detours. I've traveled that road many times and black river mud that's sticky as gumbo will suck down buggy wheels to the hubs."

He took a deep breath. "Anyway, it was a nice, sunny day and nothing happened until we were maybe ten miles south of here. Then we came upon one of those low places with a quagmire of standing water and mud. I could see tracks and ruts where other wagons and horses had passed around it on higher ground, making their own detour. So I turned off to follow the new path. The horse was picking his way between thick stands of oaks and cottonwoods, when two men rode up out of the woods on horseback, and commanded me to stop. I didn't see them coming until they were right on us."

"Can you describe these men or their horses?" the sheriff asked.

The judge paused, staring at nothing. "I was so startled, I wasn't paying much attention to details. The horses were sorrels or bays, I'm not sure which. One of them had a white blaze on his forehead — kind of a triangular shape. The riders were wearing flour sacks over their heads with eyeholes and mouth holes cut in them. No hats. Rough clothes. They pointed pistols at us. I was alarmed and put my hands in the air. I told them I had only a few silver dollars in my pocket they could have. I make a habit of not carrying much money when I travel. I asked them not to hurt us. I even told them they could have the rig."

"Anything unique about these men you recall? Voices? Mannerisms?" Stiles asked. "Wearing any rings?"

"They wore vests, but no watch chains. Nothing special about the saddles, no silver

80

trim or fancy stamping — nothing like that . . ."

"Might have been rented or stolen," the sheriff put in. "Go on. All this was in bright daylight?"

"Yes. It was afternoon, but the sun was still high. We were in the shade of the trees."

"And then . . . ?"

Zane saw the judge's Adam's apple move up and down as he swallowed.

"They said they didn't want my silver dollars. They knew Becky's name and said she was coming with them. I was horrified, and begged them to take me instead. They laughed. The shorter man had a very evil-sounding, oily kind of laugh. Or maybe that was my imagination. Anyway, they forced her to climb down. She was in tears and pleading, 'Please don't let them take me,' but I was helpless to stop them. She did not scream or cry aloud and I was proud of her for that."

The judge paused, biting his lip. He took a deep breath. "The taller of the pair dismounted and helped Becky into the saddle. Then he pointed at her bag in the buggy. 'Is that her valise?' he asked, and told me to hand it to him. The man speaking had a very deep voice. The mouth hole in his mask was cut large enough that I could see he had a heavy black mustache. He seemed to be the leader of the two. Becky wasn't equipped for riding astride, and her dress bunched up around her legs. The stirrups were too long for her, but the tall man put his foot in one of them and climbed up behind her. 'Where are you taking her?' At that point I was having trouble keeping up a brave front."

"What then?"

"The shorter man kneed his horse forward and handed me a folded sheet of paper. I opened and glanced at it as he started speaking. I don't know that I'd ever heard his voice before, but his speech was that of an unlettered man from this region. The paper was a ransom note." He paused and tossed the paper on the table before him. No one picked it up as the judge continued. "Basically, he told me the same thing that's in that note, but in more detail. He said Becky would be released unharmed provided I delivered $12,000 in gold coin to them." He paused. "But what he said next is what stunned me. And that's why you boys are here," he said, pointing at Tom and Huck. "The kidnapper said the money *had to* be delivered in person by Tom Sawyer and Huckleberry Finn."

The two boys looked their astonishment

at each other without speaking.

Tom and Huck and Jim put great store in Providence. Zane had yet to be convinced an overriding Intelligence was guiding events. But if it was, Providence had thrown an iron rod into the gears of the machine that was driving their trip to the territory.

CHAPTER 7

"The bags of money must be left in a hollow tree at the head of Eagles Nest Island anytime on Friday before midnight," the judge said.

"Eagles Nest Island?" The sheriff arched his white eyebrows.

"It's down south toward St. Louis, near the confluence of the Missouri," the judge said. "I've already asked the steamboat pilot of the packet that's tied up at the landing right now."

"Will the exchange for the girl be made when they pick up the ransom?" Stiles asked.

"No. They said they'd hold her hostage until they're safely away. They didn't say how long or where she'd be released."

The sheriff frowned. "In other words, we're at their mercy, and must trust them to free her wherever and whenever they choose."

"Can't we hold the gold until we have Becky back?" The judge was almost pleading.

"We can't negotiate because we have no way of communicating with them," Stiles said. "They'll likely be watching that hollow tree and if they see anyone around, they won't show themselves."

Silence fell.

The sheriff snatched up the ransom note and examined it. "This is regular notebook paper, and block print with pencil. No more information on here beyond what you've told us. No way to trace this."

Tom cleared his throat. "Why do they want me and Huck to deliver the gold?"

"A good question," the judge said. "I thought maybe you could shed some light on that. You boys haven't been up to some of your pranks, have you?"

"No, sir. We don't know nothing about this," Tom insisted. "We'd never do such a thing."

Huck nodded his agreement.

"What thing might that be?" the sheriff asked.

"Uh . . . *anything* that might endanger Becky or — you, judge," Tom stammered.

"Are you sure this is not some practical joke you boys concocted to stir up everyone and scare this village half to death, just for your own entertainment? Like that time you ran off and let everybody think you were drowned, only to show up at your own funeral?" The judge's deep voice rumbled, lightning flashing behind his dark looks.

The pair of former miscreants across the table shrank in their chairs.

At that moment, Zane was grateful to be a stranger.

"No judge, it warn't us — honest Injun," Huck piped up in a weak voice after a few moments of terrible silence.

"Honor Bright?" the judge pressed.

"Honor Bright!" Tom affirmed.

"Well, somehow or other these two criminals must know *you*," the judge continued. "And why the figure of 12,000 dollars? Why not $10,000 or $15,000 or even more? Not only do these kidnappers know you boys, they also know the exact amount of the treasure you found two years ago."

"Then it's likely a couple of jackleg robbers who live around here," Sheriff Stiles said.

"Not necessarily," the judge said. "All that business was in the papers up and down the river, and beyond. Anybody could have picked up the details from those printed articles."

"Couldn't be nothin' to do with Injun Joe," Tom said. "He starved in the cave." The color had returned to Tom's face and he leaned forward in his chair, once more the eager detective.

Zane and Jim hadn't spoken. They were the outsiders here, Zane thought. This was serious business and he was only an unwilling visitor. He sipped his coffee; it was lukewarm. And his pancakes were untouched.

"Judge, we don't have much to go on," Sheriff Stiles said. "I'll order my deputies to scout around this town to see if we can pick up any clues — maybe find out who's been missing for a few days, any suspicious strangers or activities, that sort of thing. But these kidnappers could be anywhere. There have been a lot of men leaving for California lately." Stiles shrugged. "Who knows, it could even be a couple of characters who didn't make it in the gold fields, and came back here looking to make their strike locally. I'd like to know what their motive is in insisting these boys deliver the money."

"I'm guessing it's to keep adult, armed law officers away," the judge said. "Less danger to themselves when they retrieve the ransom."

The sheriff gnawed thoughtfully on the corner of his drooping mustache. "I'm not so sure. There's a connection between the amount of the ransom demand you pointed out, and these boys. This is *their* money being taken; your daughter is only their means of acquiring it. I wonder if this involves some kind of a personal grudge or revenge." He focused a searching gaze on Tom and Huck. "If you boys are holding back anything that might shed some light on this, now's the time to spit it out."

Silence.

"All right, then, we must form a plan of action to deal with their demands," Stiles said. "Judge, this young lady is your daughter. What do you want to do?"

"Pay the ransom," Judge Thatcher said without hesitation. "Her life means infinitely more than any amount of money — mine or theirs."

Tom and Huck glanced at each other in some kind of silent communication. "Judge, you can use our money," Tom said, apparently speaking for both of them.

"I'm sorry, boys, I truly am. If there was any other way . . . But, except for your gold, I don't have that much."

"We didn't have nothin' when we found that treasure," Huck said. "We was gonna

88

ask you for some o' that money, directly, but I reckon Providence has other plans for it now."

"Don't you worry," Judge Thatcher said. "I'll pay you back if I have to sell this house and my farmland. Consider this only a loan."

While the discussion progressed, Zane decided not to waste the food that had been placed before them. He forked three flapjacks onto his plate, smeared them with melting butter, and drowned them in maple syrup. Let the others talk; he'd continue the process of putting on a few pounds. He added two fried sausage patties to the pile.

"How much did you tell that reporter who was here earlier?" Sheriff Stiles asked.

" 'Most everything," the judge said. "Except the part about Tom and Huck. I reasoned the more information the public knew, the better chance we had of someone coming forth with some information that might help."

"Good idea to keep the boys and the place of the drop a secret. We don't want to jeopardize Becky's safety."

Zane spoke up for the first time, talking with his mouth full. "We don't have long to raise the money. This is already Tuesday."

"Who are *you*?" the sheriff asked as if

noticing Zane for the first time.

"This is Zane, a new friend of ours," Tom spoke up quickly. "His folks are visitin' kin up north in Iowa for a spell. His pap is gonna come pick him up later."

"Hmm . . . Well, keep your mouth shut about all this," Stiles cautioned. "That goes for the rest of you, as well," he added, taking in Jim. "All the details will leak out soon enough."

"We'll keep mum."

"The new kid is right, Judge. There ain't a lot of time to raise that kind of cash in gold."

"No worry about that," Judge Thatcher said. "The market where I had their money appeared in imminent danger of collapse. I withdrew it all and converted it to gold to hold its value while searching for a better, less risky investment. It so happens that it's all here, locked in my safe."

"I wonder if the kidnappers knew that?" the sheriff mused.

"I don't know how they could have," the judge said. "There are some things in life that can only be attributed to coincidence."

Or to Providence, Zane thought. He could hardly fathom how quickly he was becoming acclimated to this new world and way of thought. He wondered how much this $12,000 was equivalent to in currency of his own day. Certainly, a vast sum.

"We could arm the men of the village, and request the help of the St. Louis police who are local to that island," Stiles said. "We could be lying in wait for them when they come to pick up the ransom."

"Oh, please no!" the judge said. "Anything could go wrong. And I want Becky back safe. Let them have the gold. We can go after that later once Becky is safe at home."

"All right. You're calling the tune here," Stiles said. "Next thing to find out is if Tom and Huck are willing to deliver the ransom as ordered."

"You bet we are," Tom enthused.

Huck nodded.

"This is not some kind of lark, boys," the sheriff cautioned. "A girl's life is at stake here, and maybe yours, too. But why in the world they want you to deliver it, I can't figure."

"Maybe 'cause of our repertation for bein' brave and bold," Tom said, his brashness returned.

Stiles shook his head. "Not likely." Then he looked thoughtful. "But I must have the permission of your parents."

"I think I can tell you what the Widow Douglas will say," the judge stated. "Tom's Aunt Polly might take a little persuading, but she'll give in when she knows Becky's life is at stake. After all, her Tom saved my Becky once before by bringing her out of that cave alive."

"Yes, that's so. I'd forgot these boys don't have parents — only guardians."

"And not even legal guardians, at that," the judge said. "These two lads were taken in. But no real parents could be better. I know these two women well. They will give their consent." He beamed at the boys.

"So that's two of our problems out of the way," the sheriff said. "The gold is available, and the boys are available." He stood and slid the still unlit cigar into his shirt pocket. "Well, I'm off to my office. I'll set my deputies to combing the area for clues about these men." He moved toward the doorway into the front parlor, then turned back. "Judge, you been up all night. After some sleep, things will look a little better. You're hurting right now. Buck up. We'll get your daughter back safe, never fear. Then we'll work on catching those criminals."

The rest of them rose to leave as well, but the judge called Tom and Huck back. "There's some extra cash in my safe I want to give you boys," he said quietly.

"What for?" Tom asked.

Zane watched and listened from across

the room. Jim had started for the front door.

"It's three hundred," the judge said. "A goodly amount and it'll tide you and your families over until we can recover the ransom." He pulled aside a framed print of a pastoral scene, revealing a wall safe.

The judge pulled out a leather pouch and counted out a pile of coins, splitting them between Tom and Huck. "I feel very bad about taking your money," Zane heard him say. "Consider this as advance interest on the loan of $12,000. Put it in a safe place until all this business is over. Maybe give it to your Aunt Polly and to the widow for safekeeping and expenses."

The boys dumped the handfuls of shiny coins into their pants pockets. As Tom and Huck walked past him on the way out, Zane saw their side pockets sagging with the weight of heavy metal.

CHAPTER 8

The four of them left the judge's house and struck back downhill toward the main part of the village. They formed a somber, silent group.

"Well, it looks like our adventure to the territory has been postponed," Zane said, trying to liven up the mood. He had no idea what territory he was even referring to.

"Yeah," Tom said, shortly.

In less than a day, Zane had learned enough to guess Tom was mentally jumping ahead, working out the details of their mission and had already forgotten his earlier plan.

"How we gonna do this, then?" Huck asked. "Eagles Nest Island's 'most of a hundred miles downriver. Me and Jim must o' passed it on our raft. We might of even camped on it, but I don't have the foggiest notion where it is or what it looks like."

"If you starts now, mebbe you be dere by

Friday," Jim said.

"You two muggins're purely lackin' any sense about this," Tom said. "We can't take a small boat. We'd never find it. There's a slew o' islands and towheads and swamps between here and St. Louis and most o' them look a lot alike — as you found out last year."

"I know you likely conjured up a plan," Huck said. "Let's hear it." The words were sarcastic, but the tone was not.

"Only thing we can do is take a steamboat and ask to be put off on Eagles Nest Island."

"Everybody on that steamboat would right soon find out what we was about," Huck said.

"All dat gold be mighty temptin' fo' anybody like de king and de duke," Jim said.

"That's why we have to keep quiet about what we're doing," Tom said.

"How you gwine to do dat," Jim asked, "when you be carrying two heavy satchels on de boat?"

"We'll have to disguise it some way," Tom said.

"Remember when we found all those coins hid in the cave?" Huck said. "We had to split it up into smaller sacks to even carry it to our skiff and back to the village. Then we borrowed a little kid's wagon to haul it the rest of the way. So even if we stash it in carpet bags, we'd look like we was tryin' to tote two elephants."

"The way the news spreads around in this village, everybody will know what you're doing long before Friday anyway," Zane said. "Why don't you carry it on board in two or three canvas bags and ask the captain to lock it in the safe — if he has one for passengers' valuables."

"I reckon that would be best," Tom nodded. "But there's another worry."

They looked their curiosity at him.

"How we gonna make it off the island after we drop the gold in the hollow tree?"

"The steamboat, of course," Huck said. "They'll wait for us. It ain't gonna take but a couple minutes — not even as long as it takes to wood up."

"That's *if* we can find the right tree that fast," Tom said. "I reckon Eagles Nest Island's slathered with trees — thicker 'an hair on a hound's back. How do you reckon somebody come to name it that? Eagles don't build their nests in bushes."

Zane had never seen a bald eagle in the wild, but learned in school they'd been saved from near extinction when the government banned the use of a deadly pesticide in 1972. The national bird was making a comeback in his time. But they were bound to be much more numerous here in the year 1849. Instead of thinking these boys lived in a backward time, Zane was beginning to like certain things about their world.

"The kidnappers must have scouted this island," Zane put in. "If a tree's hollow, it's normally dead. If it was hard to find, they'd have told the judge that. I'd bet it's pretty obvious somewhere at the head of the island."

"All right, supposin' we make the drop, and climb back aboard the steamer," Tom said. "What next? Where's the boat headed? Why St. Louis, of course, then Memphis, Vicksburg, and all points south to New Orleans. We don't wanta go to any o' them places."

"We'll hop off in St. Louis," Huck said. "We can catch the next boat north."

"While we're ridin' around, enjoyin' ourselves, where is Becky all this time?"

"De robbers got her," Jim said. "De judge say dey's gonna keep her 'til dey's outa danger b'fo' dey turn her loose."

"That ain't good enough for me," Tom said. "I wanta stay close by outa sight and watch for them kidnappers to pick up the ransom. Could be we might figure some way to snatch Becky away from them. You know them kidnappers is gonna have her close by all the time if she's a hostage."

This dangerous proposal drew silence.

"That would be putting Becky's life in danger," Zane said after a few moments. "Why not wait until they release her?"

"You don't think they'd really *kill* her, do you?" Tom said. "It's a bluff. If they was caught stealing gold, they'd likely be let off with a few years in prison. But murder is a hangin' crime for sure."

"That's a risky assumption to make," Zane said, inserting himself more and more into the conversation as if he were a participant in this venture. "We don't even know who these men are, so how can we guess what they're thinking? They might already be murderers and are so desperate for money, they don't care if they kill one more."

Tom apparently hadn't considered this possibility. "Yeah, could be, I suppose."

"You reckon Eagles Nest Island is long and skinny like Jackson's Island?" Huck said. "Let's go down and ask one o' the pilots on the *Susannah*."

The packet had been there since early morning. As the four approached the landing, there were no signs the crew was preparing to get underway.

A crewman was lounging at the guards.

"When're ya shovin' off?" Tom asked.

"When she's good and ready," the young mud clerk retorted. "Shovelin' mud outa the boilers."

"We wanta talk to one of the pilots."

"They're all busy."

"You ain't even checked." Tom was growing red in the face. "Let's go," he said striding up the gangway and brushing past the clerk.

"Hey, you can't go up there!" the clerk cried, jumping up.

"Says who?" Huck shoved himself in the young man's way.

The clerk apparently thought better of challenging all four of them and moved back, allowing Jim to pass as well.

They found one of the pilots, a clean-shaven man of about thirty eating a sandwich in the main saloon.

"Yeah, I'm the pilot. Josh Logan. What can I do for you boys?" he greeted them genially, wiping his mouth and eyeing Jim standing in back.

"What can you tell us about Eagles Nest Island?" Tom said.

"That's way down south of here. What d'ya want to know?"

"Is it a huge island or only a little skinny

99

towhead? Is it near the shore . . . things like that."

Logan paused and appeared to be picturing the island in his mind's eye.

"Eagles Nest is a broad, bluff island. Stands right out in the middle, head up to the current like the prow of a ship, about three-quarters of a mile long and a thousand feet wide. Well anchored with heavy timber. Not a place you want to come running down on, pushed by a strong current in anything but good daylight and under full steam. Channel is to the Missouri side. Is that what you wanted to know?"

"Yeah. Is there a bar?"

"Sure is. At the head. Not a long one, though. When the river's on the rise, she goes underwater pretty quick."

"Do you ever stop there?"

"No need to. It's uninhabited. That's why the bald eagles like it."

"Would your captain stop for a hail?"

Logan shrugged. "You'd have to ask him. But frankly, I don't think so. I would hope not. I always give that island plenty of leeway. One evening in a storm, when it was roaring like the devil from Hades, I was at the wheel when we come down on Eagles Nest. One of our rudder blades sheared off and she wouldn't answer the helm proper.

For maybe half a minute I figured we were goners and she'd pile up on that bar. But we cleared by a cat's whisker. My heart was beatin' faster than a hummingbird's wings, I can tell you. Had nightmares for weeks."

Zane felt a chill go up his back under the sweaty shirt. He had no experience on a gigantic river like this, and had only crossed it once in a skiff with Jim rowing. But his imagination could visualize the island — a swift, heavy current ripping past on both sides, wind bending the tops of giant trees, the difficulty landing with no protected water, the threat of running aground on the submerged bar, or losing control and crashing into the bank. It would be very tricky.

Tom and Huck thanked the pilot and the four of them departed.

"Dat ain't de kinder place I wants to go foolin' wid no kidnappers," Jim remarked as they made their way down the gangway.

Zane had been thinking the same thing. "I reckon that's the reason they chose it. They don't want any company."

Tom and Huck were quiet. They had grown up here, and spent all their lives on the river and its islands. If they were sobered by the pilot's description, it must be a truly fearsome place.

CHAPTER 9

That afternoon, the *Susannah* refilled her boilers, fired up, and subsequently departed under a full head of steam for St. Louis.

Tom and Zane went home to face Aunt Polly, while Jim and Huck reported back to the Widow Douglas.

"I'm glad you're here," Tom told Zane as they approached the door of the two-story white house on Hill Street. "Aunt Polly, she'll be a sight easier on me in front of company."

Zane wondered what kind of ogre this woman would be. He knew from reading Twain's novels that she was strict, but loving, in the face of some powerful aggravation.

"Well, there you are!" a slightly shrill voice greeted them when Tom banged the door behind them. A lean older woman in a plain gray dress, hair pulled back in a severe bun, emerged from the dining area into the tiny front parlor. "About time you show yourself. You don't think nothing of worrying a body to death, out all night and the livelong day. What're all these outrageous rumors I hear? Becky Thatcher kidnapped and you gallivanting all hours, the Lord knows where." Her rapid-fire tongue paused for a few seconds as she was brought up short by the sight of Zane. "And who might this be?"

"Auntie, you said it was all right if I went camping on Jackson's Island with Huck and Jim," Tom defended himself. Before she could reply, he took Zane by the arm. "I met a new friend. This here's Zane Rasmussen. His folks is visiting kin up in Iowa and they let him come down to St. Petersburg to look up a cousin who used to live here. But the cousin has moved to St. Louis, so we met and . . ."

"All right, never mind all that," the old lady cut him off waspishly, hardly glancing at Zane. "Tell me what you have to do with this kidnapping business. I know you're mixed up in it somehow."

"Auntie, those kidnappers told Judge Thatcher that me and Huck has to deliver the $12,000 ransom Friday to an island down near St. Louis."

"What? You two?"

"Yes'm."

"Why?"

"I don't know, but that's the only way they'll set Becky free."

"Lordy! What's this world coming to? If I don't let you go, what then?"

"I reckon they'll kill her."

The old lady wrung her hands and paced toward the front window. "My lands, who *are* these men, anyway?"

"Nobody knows. The sheriff and judge figure they's after the treasure me and Huck found, 'cause it's mostly the same amount."

"I can't let you go," she said firmly. "I almost lost you before. I can't take a chance of losing you for sure this time."

Tom looked at Zane but said nothing. Zane knew an appeal would be made by Judge Thatcher and Sheriff Stiles, so Tom didn't have to plead his own case.

Instead, Tom changed the subject. "Auntie, can Zane spend the night here?"

"I hope the Widow Douglas doesn't let that scamp, Huckleberry, run off on such a fool's errand," she mused, staring out the window.

"Auntie, can my friend, Zane, stay here tonight?" Tom asked again, trying to distract the old lady.

"What? Yes, yes," she nodded. "He can have Sid's bed. He and Mary are off to your uncle's farm for the week." Then she resumed wringing her hands, her mind obviously focused on the tragedy that was occupying the rest of the village.

"Auntie, if you don't need us for the next little bit, me and Zane'll go do some fishing."

She didn't reply at first until Tom repeated himself.

"Yes, go 'long with you. This business has me that befuddled until I don't know if I'm afoot or afloat. Hardly a wonder I'm turning white-headed."

"We'll be back directly," he said, motioning for Zane to follow him out the door. "By suppertime for sure," he said as they made their escape.

The boys did spend the afternoon fishing from the bank of the river upstream of the village. They'd dug some night crawlers from a moist, shaded area in the garden behind the house and Tom showed Zane how to bait a hook, attach a lead sinker and a cork bobber, and let the bait drift along with the slight current. They managed to pull in a couple of bluegill and two small catfish. "None of 'em a size to keep," Tom remarked slipping the last one back into the river.

Then, during the heat of the afternoon,

the fish quit biting in the shallow water near the bank. The boys stretched out on a patch of grass and fell to talking.

It was a good time for Tom to pull out two ripe, juicy tomatoes he'd hooked from the garden when they'd been digging fishing worms. Though somewhat squashed from being in his pocket, they were still delicious.

Zane reflected that he was glad to have the straw hat to blunt the fierce June sun while he munched on the tomato and stared out over the broad Mississippi. He glanced at his wristwatch.

"You got somers to go?" Tom asked.

"Uh . . . no. Just a habit, I reckon."

He took a deep breath and tried to relax. It was pleasant to put the kidnapping out of his mind for a time. They talked of Tom's earlier plans for the summer, and also recalled how Tom and Huck had found the treasure. It seemed strange to Zane to hear the details from a participant after having read about it in a book. "Do you have any of those coins with you now?" Zane asked.

Tom dug into his pants pocket and produced a $2.50 gold piece and a $5 gold piece. "I hooked these from the treasure when we first found it. Carry 'em for good luck, mostly. Auntie doesn't like me to carry

106

this much money around in case I lose it or somebody robs me," Tom said. "But Judge Thatcher he lets me have some of the interest now and again when I ask him. It's a lot more than I need to buy candy and a new hoop, or a ball. But it does me a power o' good to help Aunt Polly, so she don't have to pay for *everything* — food, clothes, rent, and such."

Zane turned over the coins in his hand, marveling at how they shone in the sun. "I sure wish we had gold circulating where I come from. Gold coins were taken out of circulation back in the 1930s during the Depression."

"What's a depression?"

"A financial panic. People lose their jobs and go bumming around looking for work. Hard times. Can't say as I understand it all that well, but heard it was bad. Long before my time."

"Oh. Well, gold is best. Lots o' banks print their own paper money, but it ain't good once you travel too far away from where the bank is. And if the bank closes up, their notes ain't no good at all." He took the coins back and put them in his pocket. "But gold is always good."

"Yeah. In this day and time, I don't suppose kidnappers would demand paper bank notes," Zane said. "Tom, you think this kidnapping business is gonna work out all right in the end?"

"I have to believe it. If I didn't, I never woulda told the judge I'd go deliver the gold."

"Are you scared?"

"Oh, a little, I guess. But I can't let on. There ain't nothin' to it, really. All me and Huck need to do is drop off the steamboat, find the tree and toss the sacks into it, and leave." He pulled up his hook and saw something had taken his bait. He dug out another night crawler from the can of coffee grounds, rebaited his hook, and dropped it back into the water. "We ain't never gonna see the kidnappers or Becky, so it won't be dangersome."

"Then why do you think those criminals demanded that you two deliver it?"

"That's the onliest thing that makes me jumpy. They's some reason, but I can't figure it."

"And what about landing on that island? How do you plan to do it if the steamboat won't land you?"

"I been studyin' on that, and I have a plan. B'tween me and Huck and the judge, there's plenty o' money to buy a skiff. Or, we'll ask the captain if we can buy the yawl offen the steamboat. When we're near the island, we'll ask the captain to heave to, have the yawl put overside with me and Huck and the gold, and the steamer can go on. We'll pull the boat to Eagles Nest Island, make the drop, and then row on downriver about twelve mile to where the Missouri River joins in. Bound to be a busy village or two nearby. I think Alton, Illinois, is along there somers. We can sell the yawl, easy, and use the money to buy two tickets home."

"The way you explain it, it all sounds simple," Zane said. "Then when you're back here, you wait to hear where Becky has been turned loose, go pick her up, and the police take out on the trail of the kidnappers. Once they're caught and go to jail, you have the treasure back and everything returns to normal. Then you're back to plannin' for adventures in the territory." He paused. "Of course, it's never as easy as all that."

"I sure hope these men ain't the killin' kind. I read about kidnappers in the old days who collected the ransom, but killed the hostage anyways, just out of pure meanness."

"Don't even think like that," Zane said. "Becky's going to be fine. After all, Providence has to let me meet her while I'm here. She'll be set free." He tried to sound confident. If most people here believed in the workings of Providence, Zane thought he'd drag it into the conversation. Providence could easily be blamed for anything that was unexpected or unexplainable. "I sure wish I could come with you," Zane said. "Jim, too."

"That would likely scare 'em off," Tom said. "And they might kill Becky out of spite." He grimaced. "Wish I could lay my hands on those two right now. No tellin' what I'd do." Then he relaxed and gave a deep sigh. "But I reckon if I was riled up enough and kilt 'em, I wouldn't escape the hangman."

"It's strange what hate can do to a person."

"Can't hate someone you don't know at'all. I just hate they took Becky prisoner."

Zane had given himself an idea. "Looky here, maybe Jim and I should tail along on the next steamboat to help out if there's trouble."

"The next southbound boat ain't 'til the next day."

"In that case, why don't Jim and I come along on the *same* boat. Maybe pay the captain to stand off the island a bit to make sure the drop goes okay before the steamer heads on downriver."

"I reckon the judge and the sheriff or

some lawmen will be ridin' the hurricane deck with a spyglass to see if they can spot the kidnappers, and to keep an eye on things so's there ain't no hitches." Tom picked up a pebble and chucked it into the river. "Iffen I was one of the kidnappers, I'd make sure to stay outa sight 'til the coast was clear before I went for that treasure. Maybe after dark. We can't be supposin' these kidnappers don't have no sense."

"Will you and Huck carry guns?"

"I doubt the judge will let us. Me and Huck have a couple old pistols hid in the cave. But they ain't much account — mostly rusted up — so it don't matter. Besides, we won't see nobody, so we won't need 'em."

Zane had a strange feeling about this paying of the ransom. His gut instinct told him it would be more dangerous than Tom imagined. "Is it okay with you and Huck if I ask Jim to come along and keep an eye on you two, in case of trouble?"

Tom gave him a quizzical look. "Sure. We'll all buy tickets on the same steamboat. We'll use a few dollars of that money the judge give us. The rest of those half-eagles and eagles you and Jim can keep safe for a day or three until we're all back home. Better to have you two carry it, secret like, in a couple money belts under your clothes than to hide it somers and maybe lose it. I'll slide my share under the floorboards in the house tonight 'til we're ready to board the boat day after tomorrow."

"You got a bite!"

Tom managed to grab his neglected pole before it was pulled into the water. He gave a yank and a silvery body flashed through the air and lay flopping in the grass.

"That's a keeper!" Zane had never caught a fish that size.

" 'Tain't nothin' but a drum — a trash fish. Too bony. No good for eatin'." He captured the fish and tossed it back into the river. With a flick of its tail, it disappeared. "Some folks eat carp, bowfin, and drum," Tom said. "Jim told me he even used to boil up fish head soup. All that bilin' softens the bones and nothin' is wasted."

"I thought old Miss Watson could feed him better than that," Zane said.

"Jim warn't always owned by Miss Watson."

"Oh." Zane cringed at the thought of fish head soup.

Tom grinned. "But I reckon when you're powerful hungry, fish heads ain't no worse than chitlins."

"What's that?"

"Hog guts. Boiled or fried."

112

Zane swallowed down his rising gorge. "Some people still eat pork rinds in my world. I'm told they're nice and crisp and not too bad."

"I read somers the French eat snails, too, with lots o' sauce to make 'em go down easy-like. Lots o' stuff you're bound to get used to while you're here." Tom grinned. "It's easin' on toward suppertime. You ready to go?"

Zane followed him back to the house, thoughts of the kidnapping forgotten for the moment.

"Where's your bathroom?"

Tom pointed toward the outhouse. "Watch out for spiders."

Zane had used fiberglass portable potties at outdoor events, so using the wooden two-holer was not an entirely new experience. He knew to hold his breath against the stench until he was done.

By the time he'd washed up at the town pump and helped Tom carry two buckets of water back to the house, his appetite had returned.

Aunt Polly had boiled up a pot of white beans and a hambone. With cornbread and buttermilk, it was as good a meal as Zane had ever tasted.

CHAPTER 10

The next morning, Zane felt better than he'd felt since arriving in this strange place.

"I was surprised how well I slept on Sid's bed," he remarked as the boys headed for Judge Thatcher's house.

"Why wouldn't you sleep good?" Tom asked.

"Well, I've never slept on a bed with rope springs."

"It's the feather tick that makes the difference," Tom said. "Corn-shuck mattresses is good, too, but they rustle a lot and sometimes keep a body awake if you roll around a good bit."

The judge was in his study when the cook let the boys in.

Tom informed him what the steamboat pilot of the *Susannah* had said about avoiding Eagles Nest Island.

"That presents a problem," the judge said,

114

swiveling around in his chair to face the boys.

"I been studyin' on it, Judge, and here's what I come up with." Tom laid out his plan to rent or buy one of the yawls carried aboard, and then use that to land, allowing the steamer to proceed downstream.

Judge Thatcher rubbed his freshly shaved chin. "That might work at that — if I can convince the steamboat captain to allow it. Where would you and Huckleberry go from there?"

"I was lookin' at a map on the wall o' the ticket office," Tom said. "It ain't over fourteen miles downstream to where the Missouri comes in. We can row that easy. There 'pears to be a village or two on the Illinois side, so we can buy some grub. If we can't sell the yawl ashore, we can always sell it to some steamboat captain. Those are good boats for layin' markers and soundin' and such, so if we offer it at a fair price, we won't have no trouble sellin' it. With the money it fetches, we can buy tickets back home."

"Tom, you have a good head on your shoulders. I shouldn't wonder if you don't turn out to be a fine businessman someday. But I'd prefer, as long as you're rowing and drifting that far, you row a few more miles on down to the St. Louis landing and meet up with me and Sheriff Stiles so we'll know you're safe. Then we can dispose of the boat, or have it hoisted aboard a steamer and ride home together."

"That's a better idea, Judge. We'll aim to do that."

The judge stood up. "I'll go down to the ticket office right now and see if I can arrange it."

"Here's the money for our tickets while you're there." He handed the older man several gold coins. "That's enough for tickets for Jim and Zane too; I want them to come along on the steamboat."

"Looks like we'll all be riding," the judge said. "Sheriff Stiles and I will be aboard as well. We'll buy tickets to St. Louis." He took his black coat from the hall tree and slipped it on.

"Oh, and while you're out, Judge, would you mind buying two money belts? I don't want nobody to know they're for us. But if *you* buy 'em, they won't think nothin' of it."

"Certainly." His face grew suddenly somber. "Can't help but wonder if those criminals are mistreating my Becky."

"Judge, they'll treat her prime," Tom said, his voice full of confidence. "Iffen they

116

don't, and she comes back with even her hair mussed up, the law will hound 'em to the ends of the world."

"Yes, yes. I suppose you're right," he nodded. "It wouldn't benefit them at all to harm her." He went out and the boys followed.

An hour later, the judge found Tom and Zane sitting in the shade of a tree near the levee, whittling new pipes from corncobs. Zane had indicated he had no desire to learn to smoke, that smoking was bad for the health and had killed many people in his own day. But he was helping Tom create some new pipes for Huck and Jim. "Smokin's okay, but it don't agree with me," Tom said, blowing the scrapings out of the soft center of the cob. "So, now, I generally let it be."

"Oh, there you are, boys," Judge Thatcher greeted them as he walked up, wiping his brow, coat draped over one arm. He braced one foot on the slope of the levee and leaned an elbow on his knee, breathing deeply. "It's all arranged," he said, handing them four one-way tickets to St. Louis. "John Lackey, the agent, is a good friend of the captain of the *Millicent,* a side-wheeler that will tie up here overnight Thursday and leave out Friday morning. That boat for sure can't land on Eagles Nest Island. So, once I explained what we planned to do, and — considering the seriousness of the situation — Lackey authorized me to buy one of their two yawls for $50."

"That's a power o' money for a small boat," Tom said.

"Those are sleek, handmade, twenty-foot double-enders that row *and* sail. They sell wholesale for $30," the judge said. "I gave Lackey retail and threw in a tip for his trouble. But two men can row one o' those with ease. You and Huck should have no trouble with it." He flung down two leather money belts that were draped over his arm. "There you are."

"Thanks a lot, Judge."

"I have some business to attend to. If you need anything, I'll be at my house."

He departed into the hot sunshine.

Zane wondered if the judge thought he was buying the money belts to transport the ransom. Tom had not said they were for Zane and Jim to carry the three hundred in gold.

Early that afternoon, Huck, Tom, and Zane managed to entice Jim away from his work hoeing weeds in the widow's garden atop Cardiff Hill. The four of them slipped away into the nearby woods. They found the oak tree where Tom had played Robin Hood two summers before and flopped down on the grass in the shade.

Tom laid out his plan for them to all come along, he and Huck to deliver the ransom, and Zane and Jim as observers from the deck of the steamboat.

"You won't be away more'en a couple days, Jim," Tom assured him. "And me and Huck'll pay you double wages for whatever time o' work you'll miss. Everybody in town knows about the kidnapping, so the widow won't mind if you come along. I'll tell her you're helping."

"Da sheriff he come up to de house dis mawnin'," Jim said, "and spoke to de Missus. Dat's da fust she know about Huck havin' to deliver de ransom."

"How'd she take it?" Tom asked.

"Take it? She doan much like it, but she had to take it."

"She give me a good lecturin' when the sheriff left," Huck put in. "Told me all the stuff to do and what to look out for. But when she got done, she kinda shook her head and said to go along, that I was likely the most growed-up boy in the village awready, seein's how me and Jim had somehow stalled off the old man with the scythe all

119

last summer. We sure didn't see no such person. If he's some kin o' hers downriver I reckon he couldn't of been no worse than the king and the duke."

Jim nodded agreement.

Zane grinned, but didn't say anything.

"Mars Tom, if you and Huck scuffs up agin some kind o' trouble, me and Zane can't do nuffin' about it," Jim said. "We be stuck on de steamboat headin' on to St. Louis."

"Won't nothin' happen," Tom said. "All we gonna do is leave the gold, then pile into the boat and row away so's the kidnappers can come pick up the money by 'n' by."

"All de same, I wisht we had some way o' reachin' dat island," Jim said. "We could all travel down de river together."

"No. We have to keep it simple," Tom said. "This ain't like the time me and Huck busted you outa the cabin on the Phelps farm. We threw lotsa style into that rescue — like the old times in France."

"Dey be dat canoe I uses to fish," Jim said. "It could do wif a bit o' patchin', but we could carry dat on de steamboat, and have it handy. It's pooty light."

"That's a good idea," Zane said. "Don't regular passengers carry luggage aboard? A small canoe could be our luggage. Isn't

120

there room to tie it down on the main deck somewhere?"

The boys hashed over this idea and agreed that they all needed to be ready for any situation, including having the ability to leave the steamboat quickly. They couldn't assume everything would go as planned.

"As long as we're buying a yawl offen the *Millicent,* I don't reckon they'd mind," Tom said. "Cordwood is stacked on the main deck, so there'd surely be room for a small canoe."

So it was agreed that Jim would have his canoe ready and near the boat landing on Friday morning.

Tom gave Huck, Jim, and Zane their boat tickets. Zane and Jim each took one of the money belts, and Huck said he'd retrieve his half of the three hundred, which he'd hidden in the cellar, and give it to Jim to hold for now.

After making sure everyone knew the details of the plan, the four of them dispersed and Jim headed back to work.

"I'll pick up a small ham, corn pone, fishing lines, lucifers, and a few other needful things," Tom said as they left. "We'll be away overnight, and could be we can't buy food nowhere."

Huck joined the boys as they descended

the steep, winding trail down Cardiff Hill to town.

"Tom, I been thinkin' we need to carry a gun," Huck said.

"You mean like that old musket you had last year? Maybe t' shoot ducks with?"

"No. I mean pistols we can hide."

"Where we gonna find pistols?" Tom asked.

"I dunno."

"Ain't nobody gonna sell us a pistol or two with powder and shot without they wanta know what we's usin' them for."

"We could say they's to protect us."

"From what or who?" Tom asked. "We ain't gonna be in no danger. If we was to encounter them kidnappers, you reckon me and you's gonna shoot it out with 'em? Not likely. We could wind up bein' kilt with our own guns. Besides," he added with a hint of pride in his voice, "I *know* what it feels like to be shot, and it ain't fun."

"I'd just feel safer," Huck said, his voice sinking as he gave in. "Zane, you ever shot a gun?"

"Yeah. My dad has a .22 rifle. We've taken it out to a farm a time or two for target practice at tin cans. Then I've shot little .22s at a shooting gallery booth at the fair."

"I don't know a size like that," Tom said.

Mostly our guns is .31 to .50 caliber."

Zane knew that guns of 1849 were cap-and-ball weapons; cartridges had not yet been invented. He started to say something about that, but decided it wasn't worth all the explanation.

"Maybe I can ask Jim if he can bring a gun along," Huck said.

"He'd have to steal it. Nobody's gonna sell a nigger a gun — even if he *is* a free man."

"Jim seems like a very responsible and moral man," Zane said. "Too bad he can't buy one like any other grownup."

"That's just the way things are," Tom said. "Bein' legally free don't change nobody's attitude."

Huck nodded.

"Sheriff Stiles will have a gun," Tom continued. "That's all we need to protect the ransom money until we deliver it. Besides, we'll put the gold in the captain's safe for the few hours it will take to go a hundred miles down to the island."

"I'm agreeable," Huck said.

"Let's spend the rest of the day collectin' the stuff we'll need — maybe an old canvas for a tent, some food and such," Tom said. "I'm gonna throw in an old pair o' shoes. My feet ain't toughened up yet, and I don't want to be hobblin' around with a cut toe or bruise."

"I'll bring a pair, too," Huck said.

"Then, tomorrow, we'll have all day to fish or play or whatever we want," Tom said.

"Yeah," Huck added, "Friday mornin' we'll be on the boat and startin' for Eagles Nest Island." He appeared to shiver. "It 'most gives me the fantods thinkin' how close we'll be to them kidnappers come Friday evenin'."

"Not likely they'll be in shoutin' distance when we arrive," Tom said. "The deadline is midnight, so I'll wager they won't show 'til after that to collect the ransom — sometime before daylight when they still have some dark time to slide out without nobody seein' 'em."

CHAPTER 11

Thursday flew by for Zane. Most of the afternoon was spent on an expedition to the cave a mile or two south of town. Zane was sweating profusely by the time the three boys hiked there and then scrambled up the wooded hillside to Tom and Huck's favorite entrance, an opening they had to crawl through. The boys had stored their oil-soaked torches inside to be handy as needed. Tom struck a lucifer to one of the torches and they were off, walking in single file.

The cool, winding aisles of red and yellow stone, dancing in the light and shadows of the torch, were vastly mysterious to Zane who was used to a world lit by electricity. The hot, muggy June day outside vanished in the silent, cool underground recesses. Strange formations and twisting pathways were marked with names, initials, and dates smoked on the walls. Overhead, the mighty cleft of ceiling disappeared beyond the torchlight.

"You sure you know where you're going?" Zane asked in a loud whisper. There was no need for silence, but the gloominess of the underground tunnels seemed to depress his spirits. He'd read all about this cave in Twain's novel, but experiencing it was a different matter entirely. His imagining of this place was nowhere near the reality.

"C'mon, let's show him where the treasure was hid," Tom exclaimed, taking the lead and holding his torch high.

The cool air was drying Zane's perspiration as he followed the pair. He wondered how the boys could go unerringly to a place as if traveling in daylight.

"There!" Tom stopped about thirty minutes later, pointing, and the other two crowded up beside him. "It was down under that rock, stuffed way back yonder outa sight."

"Pretty well hid, but we found it," Huck said.

Tom handed Huck the torch and knelt down to dig like a badger with his hands in the soft, red dirt. "Here's what I was tellin' you about." He held up an obsolete, single-shot pistol, full of dirt and rust. "It'd take a power o' work and elbow grease to fix this thing where it'd work again. I think there's an old cutlass down in here somers, but I don't recollect exactly where. Best to let the rust have it, I guess. We ain't been to this spot in a couple years. Time to let the younger boys have it if they form a gang."

After more extended hiking and exploration, Zane was completely turned around, with no idea of direction, so it came as a surprise when they struggled up a steep rise and found themselves at the opening where they'd entered. Tom extinguished his torch in the soft dirt and set it aside for future use. Zane was surprised how far down the sun had moved when they crawled out through the hillside hole and into the humid air of the wooded glade.

Zane leaned on the railing of the hurricane deck the next morning and scanned the scattered crowd. The *Millicent* had not arrived the night before as expected; the captain said they'd spent all night aground on a sandbar north of Keokuk.

It seemed to Zane that at least half the residents of the small village were at the waterfront. The *Millicent* had been moored for a half hour, unloading and loading passengers and freight, but was now getting underway.

An hour earlier in Tom's front parlor, Zane had turned away, somewhat embarrassed, when Aunt Polly had hugged Tom, tears in her eyes, telling him to watch out for trouble and how much she loved him for doing this noble thing to help rescue Becky. Exhibiting emotions in front of strangers was not something he was used to. Such feelings were usually taken for granted in his family.

Now Tom, Huck, and Jim stood near him watching the deckhands haul up and secure the gangway.

"You know," Zane said to the three beside him, "I've never been on a real steamboat before."

"Dat so?" Jim seemed genuinely surprised.

"Lots o' folks too poor to travel," Huck stated, apparently to excuse this lack of experience.

Zane smiled, knowing his own parents were well-to-do, but not wanting to brag about it. "No, we travel by car and airplanes and sometimes trains. In my day, I think there is only one real steamboat left in the whole country that still takes overnight passengers."

"Dat sho sounds like a mighty dull place," Jim allowed.

"When we have time I'll tell you all about

cars and trucks and planes," Zane said.

Two blasts on the steam whistle cut off conversation, and a cheer went up from the watchers ashore. The steamer's enclosed wheels began to thrash in reverse, backing the boat into the river.

Zane could barely make out the head and shoulders of the pilot through the glass windows of the pilothouse above them.

Tom and Huck had taken their two canvas bags of gold coins directly to the captain when they came aboard, escorted by Sheriff Reuben Stiles and Judge Thatcher.

The captain, Clarence Upton, a stern man with white muttonchop side-whiskers, had led them into his cabin and they watched as he locked the two bags in his safe. "I'll have an armed crewman on guard at my door all day," he told them as they exited the cabin, and he locked it behind him.

Then the captain had showed the boys to the white, lapstrake yawl, secured in its cradle on the larboard side. They had unlaced the canvas cover to stash their few items of food and fishing gear and part of a tent shelter. Jim had been assisted by a crewman in hauling aboard his sixteen-foot canoe, the boat showing some fresh-tarred patches, and seams re-caulked with pitch. The scratched and gouged canoe had been tied to a stanchion on the boiler deck out of the way of crewmen.

All of them except Jim had been too nervous to eat breakfast before leaving. But when the three-deck side-wheeler straightened up and pointed her jack staff downstream, the boys retired to the main cabin bearing their appetites. They were too late for sugar doughnuts. Breakfast was long over, but the cook managed to resurrect two leftover rhubarb pies from the previous night's dessert. That, along with coffee, proved to be completely satisfactory.

Jim's status had been explained to the captain by Judge Thatcher. But, being legally free did not change the black man's social status. Jim took his pie and sat humbly on a low stool along the bulkhead.

"Is this cherry pie?" Zane asked, digging in. "Wow, these cherries must be green; they're sour."

The boys and Jim laughed.

"Ain't you ever had no rhubarb?" Tom asked.

"Never heard of it."

"Looks like green and red stalks o' celery when it grows," Tom explained. "But a lemon is sweet and gentle by comparison. If you wanta pucker up, rhubarb's the thing to eat."

"De cook he sweetin' it up a good bit wid sugar," Jim added. "But it do make a fine dish."

Zane wasn't so sure. But, by the time he'd finished a slice, he had begun to enjoy the tang and flavor of it. His mother had never made pie or cobbler or sauce from rhubarb.

When the boys and Jim again came topside, St. Petersburg had vanished around a bend and the countryside consisted of bluffs on the Missouri side and forested lowlands on the Illinois side of the river.

They had settled in and begun to enjoy themselves for the all-day trip when Jim said, quietly, "If yo needs it, dey's a gun in my pocket." He put a hand to the side of his worn jacket.

"What?" Tom looked aghast. "Where'd you smouch that?"

Jim looked around and then lowered his deep voice. "Da widow, she keep it in de sideboard."

"I didn't know that," Huck said.

"Jes de widow and Miss Watson live dere a good while — two women wif no protection, she say. Case o' burglars and any other trash comes 'roun' de place."

"Did she let you have it?" Zane asked.

"Ah pays a dollar rent."

"But she don't know you took it?" Tom

131

guessed.

"Ah lef de dollar in de drawh."

Zane chuckled at the evasion. He was curious to see the gun. He looked around to make sure nobody was nearby on the deck. The deck was nearly deserted except for a couple strolling at the far end. "Let me take a peek at it."

Jim eased the pistol out far enough for the boys to see it for a few seconds behind his hand. Then the weapon disappeared again.

"Looks like a .31 caliber Colt Baby Dragoon," Tom said. "Ivory grip."

Zane looked at him in surprise.

"I was studyin' up on weapons and armor when my pirate gang was raidin'."

"Is it loaded?" Zane asked.

"Sho is. But ah don't know how fresh de powder is," Jim said. "She only a five-shooter."

"Five chambers?"

Jim nodded. "You wants to shoot mo' den dat, yo be obliged to load up wid mo' powder, balls, and caps."

Later that day, after several weary, monotonous hours of steady river travel, the morning excitement died down. Tom and Huck were slumped in chairs on the hurricane deck, seeking the shade as the bends of the

132

river threw the sun on them and then off again. The enclosed side paddle wheels churned the water to foam.

In midafternoon, an upbound boat passed them on a wide bend. The boats greeted each other with blasts on their steam whistles. Passengers waved, though the distance between boats was too great to see faces.

Zane stood at the rail watching the scenery slide smoothly past — sandbars, heavily wooded islands, and towheads thick with willows. Brooding cypress trees stood in sloughs of still water, the trackless swamps extending back out of sight in the tangled vegetation. He shivered, wondering if these swamps contained water moccasins or even alligators. He wasn't sure if the fearsome gators lived this far north.

A cabin had been reserved for Zane and Jim to St. Louis. After lunch, Jim went below for a nap, but Zane was too intrigued by his new experience of steam-boating to shut himself into a cabin. He used his time to explore.

He was amazed how quiet the pistons of the steam engine were compared to the pounding diesels of his own day. He could stand very near the steam engine and listen to the sighing as the connecting rods made their long strokes. No violent explosions that needed to be muffled. The only noise at all — and it wasn't loud — was escaping steam through a pipe on the hurricane deck.

Exploring the glass-enclosed pilothouse, Zane stood outside the open door and marveled at the red leather of the benches, the gleaming brass spittoons, the giant, spoked wheel, half sunk into the deck but still as tall as the helmsman, the magnificent view of the river from this height, the nonchalance of the white-shirted pilot, steering this behemoth with apparent ease. Two well-dressed men were seated inside, smoking cigars and talking. Zane didn't presume to enter or interrupt their conversation. From what they were discussing, he guessed they were also river pilots, perhaps deadheading, as his father had showed him airline pilots sometimes did.

Was this really America of the mid-nineteenth century? And if so, did that mean he was actually here, or only dreaming about it? As he turned away and went down several steps to the hurricane deck, he again questioned this business of traveling back in time. Tom and Huck had not brought it up recently, but he guessed they were also uneasy about this mystery — science or magic?

The brass bell clanged, signaling a change

134

of the watch. Two minutes later, the relieved pilot came down the steps.

"Do you know when we'll reach Eagles Nest Island?" Zane asked as he passed.

The lean man paused. "Late afternoon, I'd estimate," he said, stroking his drooping mustache. "Sometime after six o'clock. The spring high water hasn't receded yet, so we've skimmed over some bars we'll have to sound for later this summer. We been pourin' on steam all day to make up for time lost near Dubuque when the boat was aground for several hours. We should have arrived at St. Petersburg last night."

"Does the boat run at night?" Zane asked, since the man seemed amenable to conversation. "This is my first trip on a steamboat," he added.

"Not usually, especially running downstream, or in overcast weather. Bright moonlight is bad, too, since it creates deep shadows. We usually tie up somewhere near a woodyard."

"Think we'll make St. Louis before dark?"

The pilot nodded. "If we don't waste any time. Shouldn't be full dark until around half past eight. But we need to arrive there earlier if we can. Since that devastating fire last month, space at the landing is at a premium."

"What fire?"

"You didn't hear about that?"

"No."

"Yeah. Fire broke out on the *White Cloud*. The boats were all packed together, guard to guard, along the waterfront, and the fire spread fast. Burnt up twenty-three boats and fifteen city blocks."

"Wow!"

"City's been scramblin' to clear away the wrecks and rebuild, but there ain't nearly as many berths at the landing now, so we'd best be nosin' in there early to claim a spot."

"Thanks a lot."

The pilot waved and clattered down the iron steps toward the boiler deck.

Zane glanced at his wristwatch — 4:11 p.m. If the *Millicent* was in such a hurry, there was no chance the captain would wait for Tom and Huck to row to the island, deliver the ransom, row back to the steamer and allow the crew to retrieve them and the yawl.

Of course, that wasn't the plan from the beginning, but Zane had hoped the boys wouldn't need to be left on the island. That hope was now dashed; the *Millicent* would back water only long enough to launch the yawl and then be on its way. Every minute counted. And, judging from the amount of cordwood stacked on the deck below, the boat would not have to stop and wood up this side of St. Louis.

With these things on his mind, Zane wandered absently toward the stern and joined the boys who were stretched out on canvas deck chairs. He flopped down on a vacant chair, took off his glasses, snapped them into the case that fit snugly in his deep shirt pocket. He was far-sighted and didn't really need his glasses except for reading or close-up work. He never wore them when playing sports.

He took a deep breath of the fresh air and relaxed. He wasn't used to wearing a money belt, and the leather pressed its hard ridge against his back. But he ignored it, and it wasn't long before the soft breeze and the quiet afternoon lulled him into a doze.

CHAPTER 12

Sometime later, the change of tempo in the paddle wheels woke Huck. He sat up in his deck chair fisting sleep from his eyes, trying to bring himself back to the present.

A strong, steady wind was blowing across the exposed hurricane deck, ruffling his hair and shirt. Billowing white clouds towered into the western sky like mountains of snow. But, beneath, barely above the tree line, the sky was dark and heavy as an anvil.

Tom and Zane were standing by the starboard rail as the paddle wheels slowed, stopped, and then reversed, slapping lazily at the river to hold the boat steady against the current.

Huck jumped up and sprang to their sides. "Must be Eagles Nest Island," Huck said, pointing. Downstream nearly a half-mile, an island breasted the current, showing a solid green wall of trees more than a hundred feet tall. It looked like Huck had pictured it from the description. A slight chill went over him, and he reckoned it wasn't due to the sudden drop in temperature.

Jim appeared at the head of the stairs and came over to join them.

Two or three passengers who hadn't retired below to shelter from the threatening weather were looking downstream, apparently wondering why the boat was stopping.

The short stocky mate, John Carlson, strode up. "There she be, boys. Best collect your gear. Pilot's swinging us a bit so we can launch the yawl on the lee side." He signaled two roustabouts to man the secured lines on the davits.

"We'll see you two in a day or three," Huck said, grippng Zane's hand and then Jim's. Tom did the same. "Keep those money belts buckled tight," Tom cautioned in a low voice.

Huck felt a sudden reluctance to leave, but tore himself away. He and Tom trotted to the forward end of the Texas. They nearly bumped into Captain Upton, who was unlocking his cabin door. Judge Thatcher and Sheriff Stiles were there with him.

Without a word, the captain opened the floor safe and delivered one canvas bag of coins to each boy. Huck marveled again at the weight of the small bag — at least twenty pounds, he guessed.

"Good luck, gentlemen," the captain said, gravely, shaking each boy's hand.

"Deliver that quickly and we'll see you downriver," the judge said. "Look for us along the St. Louis waterfront. The sheriff and I will stay close by the landing until we see you and then we'll sell the yawl and all return to St. Petersburg by steamboat."

Huck nodded, a lump in his throat. He and Tom went down the companionway to the main deck and waited by the larboard side as the falls were loosened and the yawl came slowly into view from above. To keep his mind occupied, he wondered why the boats were cradled on the hurricane deck. Then the obvious answer hit him: if they had to be used as lifeboats in an emergency sinking, the yawls could be cut loose and floated off the upper deck at the last minute when the rest of the vessel was submerged.

The boat struck the water with a light splash. Two crewmen appeared beside them and unhooked the falls, then held the boat until the boys heaved the bags of coins into the bottom and climbed in after. Huck pulled on his old shoes and tied them. Tom slipped his feet into his shoes on the floor-boards.

Huck carefully pushed the boat away from the side of the steamer with an oar. Taking seats on the thwarts, one behind the other, they unshipped their oars, and took a few strokes to row clear.

The pilot, far above, raised his hand in salute and the portside paddle wheel began to slap the water at half speed.

"Shoot for the upper end and we'll ground 'er on the bar!" Huck cried above the rising wind.

Tom nodded and the boys settled to their work, stroking in unison. Even with only two oarsmen, Huck was surprised how the yawl responded and knifed through the short chop being thrown up by the stiff wind countering the current. This was nothing like the cumbersome raft he and Jim had handled. It was as fast and easy to handle as a canoe.

The boys were rested by a day of idleness. With their backs to the wind, but slightly aided by a four-mile-per-hour current, they worked the yawl down toward Eagles Nest Island.

Seconds later Huck saw a flash of lightning reflect from the back of Tom's shirt. Then the celestial artillery burst over them in booming waves, drowning all other sound. He glanced to his left. The sun had disappeared, swallowed up by a solid black mass — a typical thunderstorm buildup in the heat of late afternoon. Huck ground his teeth as he heaved back on the oar handles. Why today, of all days? He could have done without this. *Providence is kicking a few bricks in our path to see if we'll stumble.* Maybe this errand had been too easy from the start.

C'mon, faster! Maybe we can reach shelter before this hits. He picked up the tempo. Tom sensed it and increased his stroke. Drops of spray flew off their oar blades.

The sleek white yawl skimmed over the waves and Huck looked over his shoulder a minute later, surprised to see they were nearly keeping pace with the steamer that was passing the island on the Missouri side, oil lamps and torches lit, firebox doors open, resembling a giant firefly in the gloaming.

Ahead of their own boat, the sandbar was rushing toward them. For the last ten yards, Huck laid on his oars and let Tom drive the prow up onto the sand.

They clambered out and pulled the boat higher. Nobody in sight.

"Let's find the tree first," Huck said,

smelling the rain on the westerly breeze. It was coming fast.

The boys ran toward the tree line where the tangled driftwood and underbrush blocked access to the forested interior.

"Here!" Tom yelled.

A dead tree, bleached white, was half buried in the sand, canted over at a severe angle. Chest high was an oval opening.

Huck saw immediately it was the only tree around that fit the description. He dashed back to the boat and grabbed a bag of coins. Tom snatched up the other and threw it on his shoulder. They staggered through the soft sand toward the dead tree.

Up close Huck realized the opening was higher than he'd guessed. He was taller than Tom, but still had to heft the bag over his head with both hands to reach it.

Bang!

His heart gave a mighty leap and he jumped back, dropping the bag. A bolt of lightning had struck the tree, throwing chips of wood. He turned to shout at Tom when he saw two men and a girl approaching, one of the men holding a gun. Not lightning, he suddenly realized — a lead bullet had struck the tree three feet from his hands.

Tom let his bag fall to the ground. Huck was stunned, frozen by surprise and fear.

"Grab the gold," the man holding the pistol said to his companion. The shorter man ran forward.

The kidnappers had sprung the trap, Huck thought as he and Tom backed away several steps. The man picked up each bag by its tied top and waddled awkwardly with the weight. Neither man wore a mask.

"Throw 'em in our boat," the gunman ordered, then shoved the disheveled girl ahead of him as they came forward.

"Becky!" Tom cried.

She tore loose from the grip on her arm and ran to him, throwing her arms around his neck with a strangled cry. "Oh, Tom, I'm so glad to see you!"

"Are you hurt?" Tom asked, his voice muffled by her blond hair.

"No, no." She hugged him convulsively. "I never thought I'd see you two again."

"Okay, enough of that!" the gunman snapped. "Stand away from him."

Becky backed off.

"You two — this way!" the man ordered.

With the broad-brimmed hat and the dark storm clouds, Huck could make out nothing of the man's face except the fact that he had a thick mustache.

"Where?" Tom asked.

"Over there." The tall man pointed with

144

his long pistol barrel toward the west side of the sandbar.

Huck began walking in that direction.

Tom followed, holding Becky's hand.

On the downslope of the sandbar, they spied a boat drawn up close to the tree line. It was a flat-bottom riverboat about eighteen feet long, square at both ends. The shorter man placed the bags of gold under the middle thwart.

Huck's stomach began to knot up. His joy at seeing Becky was tempered. Were they about to be shot and thrown into the river? Why didn't the kidnappers take the ransom and leave the three of them?

"You two — into the boat!" the tall man ordered.

The three looked at each other. *Who did he mean?* Huck wondered. *Tom and Becky?*

"You boys, into the boat!" the man ordered again.

Huck cringed. What was this?

With the prodding of the pistol barrel, Tom let go of Becky's hand and stepped toward the boat.

The shorter man grabbed Huck and flung him at the boat. Taken by surprise, Huck stumbled on the gunwale.

The tall man looked away from Tom at the disturbance, and Tom grabbed the

145

man's gun arm, gripping it with both hands and thrusting down.

The cocked hammer fell with a deafening explosion. The man's free arm crooked around Tom's neck and yanked him back in a choke hold. The smaller man jumped in to help.

"I got this one!" the tall man yelled. "See to the others."

Huck scrambled up, grabbed an oar, and swung it. The flat of the blade smacked the smaller man on the side of the head. He fell back onto the sand and Becky kicked him in the ribs. The small man gasped and rolled over, struggling to get up.

But the taller one threw Tom aside and fired at Huck's feet. The bullet tore up the sand, and the three young people froze.

Tom stood, massaging his windpipe. Huck realized they didn't have a chance. They had to submit before one of them was shot.

"All right, no more foolishness!" the tall man said. "You boys sit down in the back of the boat. You — Becky — over there."

A crash of thunder interrupted him. Huck felt a few large drops of cold rain on his face.

The shorter man untied the painter from a bush.

"Wait! See if there's anything in their boat

we can use," the gunman said.

His companion jogged toward the head of the bar.

A minute later he returned with a sack in hand. "A ham and fishing lines, lucifers — some other stuff." He flung the bag into their punt and climbed in after it.

The tall man shoved the bow of their boat back with a booted foot.

"What about me?" Becky asked in a querulous voice.

"There's a boat — go home!" He pushed the punt into the water and climbed in, handing his gun to the shorter man. "Here, keep guard on them boys. I'll row." The boat swung into the current and he dropped the oars into the oarlocks.

Huck looked back at Becky thirty yards away, her dirty dress showing as a white blob in the gloom. He couldn't distinguish her face.

"Becky! Take our boat and go downriver!" Tom shouted. "Hail the first steamboat you see!"

"Shut up!" The man facing him struck him across the face with the pistol. Tom reeled, blood showing from a gash on his cheek.

Becky didn't move.

A wicked stroke of lightning struck a giant tree on the island and lit up everything in sharp detail for two heartbeats.

If Becky replied, her voice was lost in the thunderous boom that followed. This time, the storm burst with all its fury and a solid wall of rain roared across the river, engulfing them.

Momentarily blinded by the lightning flash, Huck could see nothing but brilliant light for several seconds. By the time his vision cleared, the boat had been carried past the tree line and Becky was lost from view.

CHAPTER 13

"Zane, dat's a gunshot!" Jim said, as the two of them headed for the stairs and their cabin on the boiler deck.

"You sure? Maybe it's thunder."

"No. I knows de sound o' guns," Jim insisted.

Zane had heard nothing of the kind, and was inclined to think the man was so keyed up that he was imagining things. But Zane's main concern at the moment was taking refuge below, beyond the frequent lightning strikes.

A minute or so later Jim was opening the shutters of their stuffy starboard side cabin to the cooler outside breeze.

Bang!

This time both of them heard the sharp report.

"That was a shot, for sure," Zane said.

"From de island," Jim asserted.

"Maybe not."

"Ain't no houses on dis stretch o' river," Jim said. "An' nobody be out a' huntin' in dis weather. Tom and Huck in some kind o' trouble, you can bet on dat."

Thunder boomed and the rain came down with a muted roar, pounding on the overhead deck.

Zane hesitated. An icy fist of fear clenched his stomach at the thought of launching himself into the blackness of that wild river and a raging storm — in an unstable canoe with no life jacket.

He looked at the white sheets on the bunk, longing with all his being to stretch out safe and dry and be soothed to sleep by the water rushing under the paddle wheels and rain thrumming on the overhead.

But even as these comforts pulled at him, he heard himself saying, "We have to go help them."

At these words, Jim sprang for the door with Zane right behind him.

Seconds later they were down on the main deck, fumbling with the ropes that secured the canoe.

"We have to tell the judge and the sheriff!" Zane shouted above the roar of the storm.

"Dey be somers on dis boat, but no time to fetch 'em."

Zane knew that Judge Thatcher and Sheriff Stiles, being responsible, logical grown-ups, would forbid them to go. Or, they would start wrangling about the wisdom of such a move, perhaps deciding to send a boat back from St. Louis in the morning and search by daylight. In any case, by the time the talking was over, the steamer would be out of canoe range of the island and the chance would be lost. Grown-ups were the same in any time and place.

Zane made a quick decision. He jumped up and ran to the nearest crewman who was stoking the firebox. "Hey, mister, me and this black man are starting back to that island in this canoe. Tell the captain we left."

Somebody had to know they hadn't fallen overboard.

The crewman paused with a log of cordwood in his hands and stared at him. Zane hoped the man understood, and delivered the message. His mind was in a whirl. Was this a virtual reality video game? If so, his thumb could punch it off the screen. But the stinging rain and his cramping stomach told him this was real.

Jim had the canoe free and was securing the long painter to a lifeline stanchion. He and Zane lifted it over and dropped it into the water.

"I gits in fust since I be de heaviest," Jim

said, one leg over the railing. "Take dis knife. When you gits in, you cut de rope."

Zane, light and nimble, had no trouble following these instructions.

Luckily, the pilot had ordered the steamboat slowed to half speed when the blinding sheets of rain suddenly cut visibility. In the several seconds it took for Zane to climb over the lines, drop into the front of the canoe, and cut the bow line, Jim was struggling to keep the canoe from bouncing against the hull of the steamer.

Jim shoved off with his paddle and seconds later the starboard sidewheel churned them out in its wake and sent them bobbing alone into the semidarkness of the Mississippi.

Zane watched with regret as the friendly lights of the steamer receded into the mist.

"Dey's a paddle in de bottom dere," Jim said.

As Zane knelt and reached for it, the wind snatched off his straw hat and sent it flying. A small matter, he thought. It was no protection. The wind was driving the stinging drops sideways with such force he could hardly open his eyes.

He felt Jim thrusting the canoe around and Zane paddled hard, working to help.

Eagles Nest Island was still visible upstream as a giant, bulky shape, somewhat darker than its surroundings.

"We gots to buck de current!" Jim shouted. "Dey ain't no slack water close by."

The west wind kept pushing them east on the choppy water, so they bent to their paddles. After what seemed an eternity, they managed to drive the canoe beyond the foot of the island into shelter from the wind. They still had to deal with the current but the water was not as rough and their job seemed much easier.

Directly, they reached the head of the island abreast of the sandbar. Rain was still falling hard, but the initial wind had passed on. Zane hopped out to ground the canoe. He saw the sky had lightened some behind the first line of storms, but now dusk was coming on.

He and Jim dragged the canoe beyond reach of the current, and Zane straightened up, panting. He thought he was in good shape, but the muscles in his shoulders and back felt strained.

They walked up onto the sand, looking around, the rain falling on their soaked clothes, cooling them from the exertion.

"They're not here, Jim."

"Dey gots to be. Dere's de boat." He pointed at the yawl beached thirty yards away.

"Probably took shelter to wait it out," Zane said. But he had no wish to plunge into the dripping undergrowth in search of them.

"TOM!" he shouted. "HUCK! Where are you?"

Jim also lifted his deep voice in a yell.

They tried again, walking slowly toward the trees, Zane knowing their shouts had to be heard by anyone within a hundred yards, even through the sound-deadening rain.

"That looks like the hollow tree they were looking for," Zane said, pointing.

Suddenly he saw movement beneath the leaning tree.

Jim jumped ahead, pistol in hand.

"Jim! Jim!" came a weak voice. A figure in white emerged from beneath the partial shelter of the dead tree and moved toward them.

Jim thrust his gun away into a side pocket. "Becky Thatcher? Is dat you, chile?"

Zane rushed forward to catch her as she stumbled in the wet sand. Her wet blond hair was plastered to her forehead, her frilly white dress hung limp, torn and dirty. She was barefoot.

"My name is Zane," he said quickly when she turned her blue eyes on him in fear. "A friend of Tom and Huck."

154

"They took them," she said as Jim came up. "Those men took Tom and Huck."

"Why?" was all Zane could think of to say.

She shook her head, weakly, wiping the rain and clinging hair from her face. "I don't know. They took the gold and the boys and let me go."

Zane felt a stab of regret. Why hadn't he insisted that he and Jim come ashore to guard them? But, if they'd done that, Becky could have been hurt or killed. These men were not fools. They had only traded one hostage for two others. But why?

"We needs to git you outen dis rain," Jim said. "Zane, you take her under dat dead tree fo' a minute whilst I see if dere's sumpin' in dat boat we can use for shelter."

Jim returned in a minute with the rolled-up canvas, and a coil of rope. "De kidnappers must of snatched de food," Jim said, unrolling the canvas shelter and throwing it over a limb that stuck out from the dead tree. He tied off the flaps of canvas to fashion a tent, of sorts. The three of them stood under it, hearing the pattering of drops and waiting for the storm to pass. Becky began to shiver, hugging herself.

"Heah's a trot line wid hooks dey missed," Jim said. "But dey took da ham and canteen and some trifles we put in dere dis mawnin.

155

Musta been in a hurry."

"I'll go look again," Zane said.

He returned with a short axe that had lain hidden under a thwart. But, aside from the oars and the unstepped mast and sail, that was it.

"Ah carries lucifers ah keep dry in candle wax," Jim said. "But dey can't start no fires wid nuffin but wet wood."

"In Boy Scouts I learned how to start a fire with wet wood and no paper," Zane said. "Look around and see if you can find some dry sticks that were protected from the wet under this mass of brush and leaves."

He took the short axe, hacked off a limb from the dead tree, and threw it on the sand under the shelter. He scraped aside the wet sand until he was down to the dry. Then he held the limb on end with one hand and hacked at it until he had a small pile of dry shavings from inside the wood.

By then Becky and Jim had returned with two handfuls of twigs that were reasonably dry. He needed some dry grass or paper, but knew he was out of luck on that score. But Jim had a small bundle of dry matches coated in wax, and by strategically arranging the tiny scraps of fuel and dry bark, Zane managed, on the third match, to ignite

156

a tiny flame. By carefully feeding it, they built up a little fire. Zane hacked off another limb from the dead tree, shaved off a layer of the outer surface, split the limb, and eventually started a blaze that could survive on its own.

"Yo's pooty handy wid dat axe," Jim said.

"Thanks. One of my few practical skills," Zane said with pride. He thought of several other talents he had that meant little in the real world of survival — tweeting, texting, manipulating video games, kicking a soccer ball.

As the fire strengthened, they piled more damp wood on, and it sizzled and sputtered and smoked, but gradually dried out and burned. They slid the canvas shelter back a couple of feet to allow the smoke to escape. By then the rain had nearly stopped — and with the coming of dusk, the no-see-ums, mayflies, and mosquitoes took over.

Zane and Jim scraped the wet sand aside to make dry spots to sit, huddling close to the flames to dry their clothing and as close to the smoke as possible to ward off biting insects.

Before darkness settled in completely, Jim took a small dip-net seine from his canoe, and managed to scoop up a few minnows to use as bait for the trot line he set out, floating it with a stick and tying the other end off to a well-anchored bush.

"I'm so glad to see you two," Becky said, when they were reasonably comfortable, the flames lighting up their faces around the small circle.

"Did those kidnappers torture you?" Zane asked, thinking of stories he'd read about such things.

"No. They didn't hurt me at all," she said.

"Where were you all this time?"

"They took me on horseback down the river to an old abandoned house off that way somewhere," she said, pointing west by north. "The place was dirty and disgusting. But at least it had been empty for so long that there weren't no rats around — nothing for them to eat, I guess."

"Did you know these men?" Zane asked.

She shook her head. "They were strangers to me."

"Did you hear their names?"

She nodded. "They called each other Chigger and Gus. I think Chigger was the short one without the mustache. He was the mean one," she added.

"Mean? How?"

"He was forever talking about the treasure and what he'd do to Tom and Huck for stealing it from him — that it was really his,

158

and things like that."

"Well, I'll be . . . So they were planning all along to turn you loose and grab the boys?"

"I suppose so."

"If dat don't beat all!" Jim said.

"Sounds like they wanted the treasure *and* revenge," Zane said. "I wonder why they thought the $12,000 was theirs to begin with?" All he recalled about this situation was what he'd garnered from his recent re-reading of *The Adventures of Tom Sawyer.* He had not lived through it as Jim had. But even Jim had not been an active participant, like Tom and Huck.

"Yo didn't know dis short man?" Jim asked.

"If I ever saw him before, I don't remember his face," Becky said, running her fingers absently through her tangled hair. "But I might have seen him around town and never paid any attention."

Zane remembered he carried a plastic pocket comb and offered it to Becky. She took it with a smile of thanks and began to rake out the snarls.

Zane continued the questions while her memory was fresh. Tom would have been proud of his detection methods.

"Did they ever talk about where they were

159

bound, once they collected the ransom?"

Becky was silent for a few seconds, staring into the fire as she paused in her combing.

"They'd have arguments when they thought I was asleep on that old dirty blanket they gave me for a bed," she said. "The tall man, Gus, wanted to head for New Orleans and then out of the country for a while. But Chigger, the short mean one, said he would start west for the gold fields — said it'd be easy to lose himself among all those Argonauts."

"Dat be pooty smart," Jim nodded.

"The man with the mustache said he'd be glad to be rid of me because I was so whiny."

"Did you aggravate them that way?" Zane smiled.

"I did all I could. But I was afraid if I carried it too far, they'd whip me. I never had a whipping in my life and I didn't want to start now. Tom took the only one I should've had in school, and now he's in their hands." She blinked away tears that formed in her eyes.

"Did Chigger ever say how he'd treat the boys to take his revenge?" Zane asked. "What he had in mind?"

"Not for sure. He was always saying things like he'd shoot their earlobes off, or pull out their fingernails, or force them to eat

160

habanero peppers, raw, to burn out their insides. He seemed to enjoy thinking up all those tortures. But I didn't half believe him, and neither did Gus. But Chigger used to brag about the things he planned to do, and laugh like he was already enjoying seeing Tom and Huck hurting."

They fell silent for a minute or two, entertaining their own thoughts.

Finally Zane said, "Jim, in the morning if you want to hide your canoe on this island we can come back for it later. Tom and Huck left a nice yawl we can either sail or row downriver to St. Louis. Then we'll try to find Judge Thatcher and Sheriff Stiles so we can take you home, Becky."

Jim nodded, but Becky was silent for a minute. Then she laid down the comb and said, "I think we should go after those kidnappers right now, without wasting any time. They can't be too far away. They wouldn't run downriver in that old leaky flat-bottom boat in the storm. When they were fixin' to come over to this island, two days ago, they forced me into that old boat and we went off into the swamps and bayous over west of here. Lots of marshes and backwater where the river overflows in those lowlands. They seemed to know where they were headed, and poled that boat to a little

161

dry island, and let me sleep in the boat I was so scared of snakes. The bugs nearly ate me up, but they didn't seem to mind the bites. Anyway, I'm betting that's where they went tonight to ride out the storm until tomorrow daylight."

"Any idea where they might go from there?" Zane asked.

"No. Don't know if they'll split up now that they have the treasure. I doubt if they'll go back to that abandoned house where they held me."

"Dey won't let go of de boys if dey figure de law be on dere tail," Jim said.

"They might each take a boy as a hostage," Zane guessed.

"That house is so isolated on the edge of the swamp, that we didn't see a soul the several days I was there," Becky said. "They might go there and wait until they think the law has lost interest or given up."

"De law ain't gonna give up lookin'," Jim said. "But if dat place be so hard to fine, dat's sho where dey might hunker down for a spell. Wif all de water roundabout to throw off de hounds, dat be a good place for runaway niggers to hide out, too."

"That reminds me," Becky said. "I did hear Gus, the tall man, say something about hunting runaway slaves. And he didn't talk like Chigger or any other man from around here."

"Dat make sense," Jim said. "A slave hunter likely be knowin' 'bout places like dat ole house. And he knows his way 'round de swamp."

"If they couldn't find that house again tonight, they might've stopped at the little dry island. That place is so deep in the marsh, I don't know how they ever located it. But the slave hunter didn't seem to have any trouble the other day. If they were able to navigate back in that swamp before dark, I suppose they could've reached it, even in the rain."

"We'll have to wait until morning before we decide what to do and where to go," Zane said. "I'm thirsty right now," he added, "but there's nothing to drink but river water."

"Dat's so," Jim said. "No cups or jugs to carry water nohow."

"And if you catch any fish on that trot line, we'll have to put them on sticks over the fire to cook them — like hot dogs."

"Dat would work, sho 'nuff," Jim nodded. "Fish is good, but I ain't 'bout to eat no dog. Mebbe we kin find a spring on dis island."

"If we're taking out after them, we can't

163

waste much time," Becky said.

"We can't rush off and get ourselves lost in the swamp," Zane said. "I want to find them as much as you do, but we should think this through. We have to notify the authorities first and tell what happened, and show 'em you're safe — especially your father. The law can do a better job than we can of finding them. Maybe the sheriff or somebody will let us tag along on the hunt." Zane had serious doubts about this, but didn't voice them. "Do you want to hunt for those criminals yourself? No fooling?" He glanced at her ragged dress and pantaloons, the scratches on her arms and gaunt face. "You've been through a lot. You're in no condition . . ."

"Mister Zane whatever-your-name-is, if I don't do everything in my power to rescue Tom and Huck, and something bad happens to them, I would regret it the rest of my life, if I live to be ninety. I'm tired of being treated like a China doll that might break. I been through enough these past few days to prove I'm strong and can put up with a lot."

Zane heaved a sigh. Girls in his time were no different.

"And you forget one important thing," she added. "I'm the only one who knows what these men look like."

"Oh, that's right. I didn't think of that," Zane said. "Okay, if you're still bent on chasing them yourself, we'll go with you." He glanced at Jim who nodded his assent. "But we need food and water, and you need clothes. Jim and I have money so that's no problem. Then the next thing is to figure out where they went or might go after they hole up for a bit."

"Mars Tom say it only be a dozen miles or so downriver to where de Missouri River jine up wid dis river. Boun' to be a village dere wid a lawman."

"That's right, Jim. We can row that distance pretty quick with the current in that nice yawl. We'll leave at daylight. Should be there in less than two hours." He pulled off his damp, itchy shirt and held it up to the heat of the flames. He'd risk the mosquitoes for a bit. He couldn't sleep in wet clothes.

"I don't want to sound like I'm ungrateful you rescued me," Becky continued in a milder tone. "I surely do. But now it's our turn to rescue *them*. The law needs me. I spent several days with those two no-accounts, and I could spot 'em a good distance off."

"Then let's try to sleep if we can and start fresh in the morning," Zane said.

The fire was burning low and they had no more dry wood.

Jim went to the edge of the bar and dragged his canoe up close.

"It ain't gonna rain no mo' tonight," Jim said, turning the canoe on its side. "Iffen ah puts dis canvas on de sand, Miss Becky kin sleep on it 'twixt de canoe and de fire and be mo' comfortable."

"Jim, you're a real gentleman."

"Zane kin sleep on de sand close by whilst I go bail out de yawl and sleep in dere wif de sail over me."

"Good idea," Zane agreed. "You still have your pistol. If a steamer comes along you can attract their attention with the standard distress signal — three shots." He'd read somewhere this was like an SOS, but had no idea if it was true.

"Onliest things wrong wif dat notion," Jim said, "is dat no steamboats be running at night in dis weather. And de powder's done wet so ah can't fire no shots."

Jim pulled down the canvas shelter and spread it on the sand, dry side up. "Long as de frogs and de crickets be aclatterin', we's safe. If dey stops, some critter or man be sneakin' roun' close by."

Zane didn't know that. As he prepared to bed down, he wished he hadn't learned it

166

now because he'd be lying long awake, listening for the croaking and chirping to stop.

Even more of a worry was a story his grandfather had told him about camping along the Tennessee shoreline of the Mississippi four summers ago. He'd heard a lot of squealing and grunting in the nearby brush during the night — unmistakable sounds of dangerous wild boars — animals with long tusks and armor-thick hides. His grandfather had lain awake all night with his hand on his revolver. But Zane doubted any razorbacks were on this island as early as 1849. Still . . .

CHAPTER 14

"I can't handle both these boys by myself," Chigger Smealey said, pausing to worry off a bite of tobacco. He offered the burley twist to the man sitting beside him, but Gus Weir shook his head. "We'll have to stick together until we're a long way off from here. Then we can split up and each go his own way." Smealey worked the chew into one cheek.

Gus Weir frowned. "New Orleans is my home port. Once I'm set up there, I can dart out of the country, quick-like, until things cool off."

The two men were sitting on the sun-warped front steps of a two-story frame house several miles west of Eagles Nest Island. The house, like the small barn behind it, was on its last legs, leaning precariously, roof partially caved in, glassless windows gaping like vacant eyes, all vestiges of paint long since blistered and pealed away, the boards weathered a dull gray.

Smealey glanced around at the house that had been their home for nearly a week. It wasn't much, but he had to give Gus credit — it was a secure hideout, nearly surrounded as it was by a treacherous swamp. The area had apparently once been a nice small plantation. But over the years, the vagrant Mississippi, twisting and turning, flooding and receding, had eaten away the banks, formed oxbows, then cutoffs, and eventually the land had been inundated with floodwaters that never receded, creating swamps and backwaters, taking most of the arable land. Whoever had farmed this place years ago had abandoned it to the elements, and to its use by the current residents, Chigger, Gus, Tom, and Huck.

The two men sat on the steps in silence for several minutes.

The midday June sun beat down in the still, humid air, and Smealey felt sweat trickling down behind his ears from beneath his straw hat and down his sides inside his shirt. He spat tobacco juice into the deep grass, then slapped at a whining mosquito too close to his ear. He could hardly wait to vacate this place, but agreed with Weir it wasn't safe to move yet. His partner had more patience than he did. So far, his own plan had worked admirably, but it had taken both of them, each contributing suggestions, to make it slide along like a slice of greasy possum on a platter. Weir was not the type of man he would want to partner with for very long. But this one project had snapped up the treasure he'd lost to those two kids inside, and once he took out his revenge on them, he'd be off to Indian Territory, or the gold rush, or somewhere far away — with $6,000 in gold.

"I'd head for New Orleans right now if I thought it was safe," Weir said. "But you can bet once that girl spreads the word to the St. Louis police, they'll be checking every steamboat, scow, and skiff headin' south for several days. A flea couldn't hop through."

"Maybe we shoulda set that yawl adrift and delayed her gettin' home for a while," Smealey said.

"Naw. She might have panicked and tried to swim ashore. That's a long way with a swift current. I didn't want the little brat to drown. Then, if somebody found her body downstream they'd think we killed her for sure. Better she arrive back safe in a couple days and tell the law we have the boys as hostages."

"She knows our faces," Smealey reminded him. "They'll have our descriptions and drawings out on wanted posters."

"That's all right. We'll mosey along in disguise for a while. Maybe travel separately, and each take one of those boys as security. I couldn't see sitting around here all week with the girl while I was wearing a sack over my head in this heat, or sportin' a blond wig or a putty nose. We can put that stuff on when we light outa here."

"So, where we headed?"

"Our best bet would be to start north into Iowa, and then join up with one o' them wagon trains striking out for the gold fields. Ain't nobody gonna be lookin' for us north and west."

Smealey thought a moment. "Council Bluffs, Iowa, is hundreds of miles from here. How we gonna get there? We have horses but that's a long way, and toting them boys along and keepin' 'em shut up all the while would take some doing."

Weir shook his head. "Too much work and risk. There's easier ways. We ain't but a few miles overland from St. Charles. We'll take a packet up the Missouri and catch a wagon train at St. Joe."

Smealey pondered that option. "I see two problems with that. First, every one o' them

Missouri riverboats is gonna be jam-packed with gold rushers. And second, don't you think the police are gonna be checking those boats, too?"

"The crowds will be in our favor," Weir said. "The law can't stop *every* boat and check *every* passenger. There's dozens of boats headed upriver daily. Besides, we'll be in disguise and we won't travel together. If we keep those boys apart, they can't hatch any mischief about escaping." Weir chuckled. "You can torture 'em a little, but not too much — only enough to put the fear o' God — and you — into their imaginations."

"What should I threaten them with?"

Still grinning, Weir said. "You'll think of something. Maybe promise you'll cut off some vital body part and let 'em bleed to death if they open their mouths. You can scare 'em into anything. The trick is, they *have to* believe you'll really do it."

"Murder is out of the question."

"*I* know that, but they don't. You can treat these boys a little rougher than that girl. After all, it was your idea to swap hostages so you could lay your hands on Tom and Huck and punish them for stealing the gold you and that breed found."

Smealey nodded. "I can handle that. They'll be beggin' for mercy before I'm

172

through. They'll do anything I say by the time we reach St. Charles."

"Okay, you have 'til day after tomorrow and then we'll leave. That'll give me a chance to work up some good disguises. There will be a half moon so we'll have a little light if we have to travel at night."

"Did you ever think you'd be wearin' chains like a slave?" Tom Sawyer asked, examining the metal shackles that fastened his hands together in front of him.

"Never in my life," Huck replied, shifting his back against the wall, and jingling the links of the chain that held his hands only six inches apart.

The two boys were sitting on the floor of an empty room in the kidnappers' hideout. The rickety house was one of the old-fashioned kind that was two stories tall, but only one room deep. Hot as it was, the upper story at least absorbed some of the fierce sun. And the back door was missing, leaving a gap in the wall for some air and also allowing a view of the waist-deep weeds and the tilting barn behind. The kidnappers' two horses were quietly grazing in the deep grass.

Tom wiped a sleeve across his sweaty face. "This place looks like it could fall down in a strong wind."

"I seen old barns leanin' like this mos' likely since Columbus discovered the Injuns," Huck replied absently, his mind apparently elsewhere.

After several seconds of silence, Tom suddenly burst out, "Wow! Hucky, that's it! That's it!"

"What's it?"

"It only just come to me!"

"It did? What did?"

"I been thinkin' all along I knew that Smealey from somers, and now I know!"

"Yeah?"

"You recollect when we was hidin' upstairs in that old haunted house and Injun Joe and his partner come in there and found our pick and shovel with the fresh dirt on 'em?"

"Lordy! I ain't likely to forget. 'Most gives me the fantods thinkin' about it. Hadn't been for them steps breakin' we'd of been found and kilt for sure."

"And we didn't know at first it was Injun Joe because he was in disguise like a Spaniard, with white whiskers and wearin' them green goggles and all?"

"Yeah, what about it? He's dead now."

"But the man who was with him *ain't* dead. His name is Chigger Smealey and he's settin' out front there right now."

174

"Oh, Lordy! How do you know?"

"I mostly recollect his voice. That face is some older and it's covered over with about two weeks o' whiskers, but it's him. I'm certain of it."

"Tom, we're in a fix for sure now. Everybody but King Arthur knows we wound up with that gold stash they discovered under the hearth that day." He brushed away a fly that lit on his nose. His hands trembled, rattling the chains on his shackles.

"It took me the longest time to figure out why them kidnappers wanted me and you to deliver the ransom. Now it makes sense. Right before they found that treasure under the fireplace, Injun Joe was talkin' about takin' revenge. He had to be meanin' revenge on us — mostly me — for speakin' out in court and tellin' how we saw him murder Doc Robinson. Now this Smealey is doin' the same because we stole his gold."

"What d'ya think he's gonna do to us?"

Tom paused for a moment, thinking. "Well, he ain't gonna kill us — not right away, anyhow. We're hostages. He'll keep us alive until he's absconded clean away from here. Then he'll either kill us or let us go."

"If he lets us go, he knows we'll go to the sheriff or a constable or somebody and tell on him."

"Yeah, but by then, he'll be long gone, I reckon."

Huck let out a long breath. "Our feet ain't tied. We need to run — now — out that back door and into the swamp. We could hide where them two won't never find us."

"He could shoot us in the back afore we was halfway across that field to cover," Tom said. "That's likely why they left our feet loose, except at night. That man, Weir, he's a nigger hunter and he knows his business. That's why he had these metal shackles. We'd die in that swamp, even with only our hands locked in front of us. Nothing to eat or drink and only the sun to tell us which way to go to the river. Water moccasins out there, too."

"Beats waitin' around to be murdered," Huck said, his face paling under his tan.

"Best we keep mum and not let on we know him," Tom said. "Maybe he won't be too hard on us. We'll pretend we're in one o' them dungeons during the French revolution and can stand the torture. Because, sure enough, we'll escape by 'n' by and justice will prevail."

"I reckon pretendin' is better than thinkin' it's really happening."

Footsteps on the porch announced the entrance of one of the men.

176

Smealey entered the room and stood with his hands on hips, regarding them. "Well, my thieving friends, how are you doing in here? Well, I hope."

"Can I have a drink of water?" Tom asked.

"Why, sure." Smealey went to a wooden bucket on the other side of the room, dipped up a scoop of water with a hollow gourd, and handed it to Tom. He emptied it eagerly.

"What about you, Mister Finn?"

"Yes."

Smealey gave him a full dipperful, then returned the gourd to the bucket.

"Precious fresh water. Now you must pay for it and for your previous sins." He reached into the pocket of his jeans and produced a small pepper that was a pale greenish orange. He broke it between his fingers. "You two seem to have picked up a few scratches on your arms and legs and neck and apparently clawed at a few mosquito bites as well." He approached them. "And what a shame it seems you've brushed up against some poison ivy or poison oak. Here, let me rub a little balm on those rashes."

He swiped the juice of the pepper into the raw thorn scratches and red insect bites on Huck's left leg and upper arm.

"Auggh!" Huck grimaced and rolled away on the floor.

Tom saw Smealey coming and kicked out with his shod feet.

The man batted them aside and slammed Tom's legs to the floor, pinning them with his knees. Before Tom could ward him off, Smealey rubbed the pepper oil into four raw spots on his skin, including the cut on his cheek where Smealey had struck him with the gun barrel the night before. The pain began slowly, but then felt like someone was holding a burning twig to each spot.

Smealey stepped back, eyes glowing, a maniacal grin on his whiskery face. "You two was struttin' around like royalty, spendin' my gold. I allow I'll take you down a peg or two. You stole my treasure, but now I have it secured again. With your help, I'll keep it, too. You two thieves think you have the law on your side. But you're our guarantee against the law laying a hand on us. When we're away into the territory and outa their jurisdiction, we won't need you brats no more. And it will be my final pleasure to dispose of you." He reached and pulled a Colt from the back of his belt, half-cocked the hammer, and turned the cylinder, examining each load as it clicked past his eyes.

Tom caught his breath at the pain of the hot pepper in his abrasions, biting his lip, but determined not to show how much it hurt, although his eyes were watering. He barely heard what Smealey was saying. But the man's next remark cut through the fog.

"Maybe I'll be back later and notch your noses. That was a favorite trick of my old pard, Injun Joe." He gave an oily laugh and left the room, banging the warped door behind him.

Gasping, Tom prayed for the intense pain to fade. How much more of this could he stand? Maybe being shot in the back trying to escape would be preferable.

CHAPTER 15

Zane pulled on the oars, synchronizing his stroke with Jim's. He'd never rowed a boat until he found himself in this place and time. And here he was, skinny arms and all, pulling a boat on the Mississippi River with this muscular black man who was doing most of the actual work. Zane and the current were combining for the rest of their propulsion. Becky had insisted she be allowed to help, but had lasted only a few minutes, as her arms were too short to stroke in rhythm with a second oarsman.

What a river this was! Zane marveled that it was wild and free to go where it would, free to flood in spring, to form and destroy sandbars, to carve away dirt banks, depositing the soil somewhere downstream or washing it clear to the gulf, to twist, forming loops and then cutting them off, making oxbows and islands.

The Corps of Engineers was still around

the bend in the future. No one had yet tried to harness the power of this water, to build any dams or revetments to maintain a channel. Steamboat pilots now were skilled artists who had to know the river, and dodge sandbars and wrecks at their peril.

Zane was beginning to enjoy this. He'd been here since Monday and, by his calculation, today was only Saturday. It seemed much longer. He had already ceased to miss his former, routine existence. His eyes now gloried in the sights of all these new adventures. It was a great summer vacation.

He and Jim and Becky had started early this morning after a hasty breakfast of hot catfish eaten with their fingers and had so far been on the water close to three hours. Zane thought he should be exhausted by now, but wasn't.

"Hold!" Jim said. By mutual agreement, they rested on their oars and drifted while they caught their breath and scanned the dark green, heavily wooded shoreline. Zane looked over his shoulder and saw a white sandbar marking an approaching towhead.

They'd passed only one upbound steamboat all morning, and had seen a few houses of a small village high on a westside bluff. The silence was wonderful and relaxing to Zane who was used to some kind of constant noise in the world he'd left — the blather of TV, muted roar of car and truck traffic, overhead jets, police and ambulance sirens, irritating buzz of lawnmowers and weed eaters, electronic bleeps from all manner of handheld devices, along with various odd rings of cell phones everywhere he went.

"This river has lots of bends," Zane observed as the current carried them along.

"Yasuh, dis be da snakenist river ah knows."

"How far you think we've come?"

"Hmm . . . 'bout ten mile. Mebbe mo'."

"Guess we need to keep a sharp lookout for Alton," Zane said. "I'd guess it's the only town of any size around here."

"Mebbe best we leaves Alton be," Jim said after a short pause.

"Why? Could be a sheriff there or a few policemen."

"Dat place be pooty bad for niggers," Jim said.

"But it's on the Illinois shore — in a free state." Zane was proud of his knowledge of geography and history.

"Dat mebbe so," Jim said. "But slave hunters cross over dere all de time, no matter what de law says. Few year ago, a mob went over dere and kilt de abolitionist edi-

182

tor. Threw his press in de river. Lots o' fights and shootin's amongst de slave holders and abolitionists."

They drifted silently for a few seconds.

"De village o' Wood River be along here somers," Jim said. "But dat be in Illinois, too. Best we stick to de Missouri side."

"Next large city is St. Louis," Zane said. "You want to shoot for it?"

"We needs water, mostly," Jim said. "St. Charles be de nearest town on de west side 'round de bend where de Missouri River comes in."

"We'll aim for that, then," Zane said, secretly glad for a closer goal. In only the few minutes of rest, his arms and shoulders were starting to feel very fatigued. Maybe he'd go back home looking like a weight lifter — *if* he ever got home at all, he thought, with a slight twinge of longing. But for now, he was free to be and do anything he wanted.

His stiffening muscles were soon forgotten as they took up their stroke again. Zane marveled at the design of this yawl. He had nothing to compare it to, but it seemed easy to row. The twenty-foot lapstrake hull had to weigh quite a bit, but it seemed to sit on the water lightly, easily capable of a much heavier load. He'd seen it hanging in the davits, and noted it had about an eight-inch-deep keel that ran nearly the entire length of the bottom, apparently to help it track straight and to keep it from sliding sideways when sailing off the wind. He and Jim had discussed whether or not to rig the sail this morning, but the prevailing wind was out of the southwest, in the general direction they wanted to go. And neither of them had experience trying to tack a boat against the wind, so they decided to row and let the current help.

Even though the rowers could determine direction, Becky sat in the stern at the tiller and steered when needed. Since Jim and Zane had to sit with their backs to the bow, Becky could watch for snags and shoal spots ahead and guide the boat around them. Only three times had they run aground on submerged sandbars and had to climb out and push the boat off.

But these were welcome interruptions to Zane. It was a glorious summer morning and he reveled in the chance to splash around in the cool water for a few minutes. His white sneakers were beginning to look pretty grungy.

St. Charles might have been closer, but it took several more hours to reach. Two things worked against them. Once they turned into the outflow of the muddy Missouri, they were struggling upstream and were also bucking a headwind. Adding to that, St. Charles was a good way up the Missouri instead of right at the junction of the rivers as Zane had envisioned. Per Jim's directions, they hugged the north shore trying to stay in the slack water. But it was still a tough slog with the afternoon sun bearing down on them, current and wind against them, and fatigue and thirst building up.

By the time they saw a fair-sized town coming up, Zane was spitting cotton. He prayed it would be St. Charles. If it wasn't, they had to stop and find some water, no matter what.

"Dah be St. Charles," Jim gasped, letting his oars drag in the water as the boat slowed. "Thank de Lawd."

They beached the boat on the muddy riverbank, tying it off to a cottonwood. All three of them sat for a few minutes, catching their breath and quietly enjoying the shade of the tree and the cooling breeze over the water.

"Jim," Zane said, "we'll be going among strangers. Do you have any papers showing you're a free man?" He was beginning to be as leery of this society as those who'd lived here all their lives.

"Ah surely do." He pulled a tattered leather coin purse from his pocket, dug out a folded document, and handed it to Zane. "Ah can't read, but ah never goes anywhere without dis."

Zane unfolded the legal size, water-stained paper that was beginning to crack in the creases due to constant wear. It had a Missouri state seal embossed at the top and was partly printed, partly handwritten; it was full of legal language, but testified to the fact that the bearer, Jim Watson (the surname of his last owner), had been duly granted his freedom by the last will and testament of Miss Emily Watson, etc., etc. It gave Jim's approximate age as thirty, a general physical description, and then a more specific identifying mark of a scar on his left shoulder. The document was signed by Miss Watson, dated fourteen months previously, and bore the signatures of two witnesses.

Zane refolded the document and handed it back. "Jim, that looks all legal and proper. Hang onto it in case anyone has a need to see it."

"De judge say dey be a copy o' dis in de cotehouse, too, 'case dis one be lost," Jim said.

"Good. But no slave hunter will bother to

check these records at the courthouse." He thought for a moment, looking toward the buildings of the nearby town. "Tell you what, Jim, I think it might be a better idea if Becky and I go into town and you stay here with the boat. I don't want anyone giving us problems when they see a black man and a blond girl and a boy who's part Chinese coming into town. Might attract some unneeded attention. Tell me where I'm likely to find water. I'll bring back what we need. I have plenty o' money."

"Don't let nobody see dat money belt, Zane."

"I won't. I'll take out a few coins and put them in my pocket."

Jim proceeded to tell Zane and Becky there was likely water at a public pump near the center of town somewhere. Or they could ask someone. Three large canteens could be bought at a general store or hardware.

Zane said he'd bring Jim some tobacco and some gunpowder and .31 caliber balls for his pistol.

"Don't forget de caps fo' it," Jim said. "Dis pistol ain't no good wifout dem."

"Will they sell ammunition to a kid?" Zane asked, thinking about the restrictions on minors where he'd come from.

"Long's you gots de money, dey don't care."

"We'll be back as soon as we can."

Zane and Becky set off walking the mile to St. Charles. She was still looking very bedraggled, and Zane suggested they stop somewhere so she could buy herself some clothes that looked better than the dirty and torn white frilly dress.

"We'll find a store and you can do some shopping."

"I've been in these clothes for several days and I feel grimy and dirty. Wish there was someplace I could take a bath."

"Well, until that happens, at least some new clothes might make you feel better."

She smiled at him, and Zane realized for the first time that she was a very pretty girl.

"Are there any part-Chinese people around here?" Zane asked.

Becky shook her head. "None that I've ever seen."

"The way people think of blacks and Indians and half breeds around here, maybe I should act like your servant if someone should stop us," he said. In this unenlightened society, he wasn't about to assert his rights, if challenged. He was all about keeping a low profile. "You pretend be the little rich girl who has a half-Chinese servant

188

your daddy sent along to help you carry your packages."

So, with this cover story, they bought three half-gallon size canteens and were directed to the town pump two blocks from the river. Here they slaked their thirst and filled the canteens. Zane slung them on his shoulder while Becky led him to a store where she could buy some clothing. It was a large general dry goods mercantile, not nearly as large as the modern discount stores Zane was used to, but crammed with all manner of merchandise, from clothing to weapons to tools, much of it hanging from the ceiling to make maximum use of space. He waited nearby, looking at the variety of goods, while she picked out a gray, mid-calf, divided riding skirt and two white cotton shirtwaists. Zane looked the other way while she and the female sales clerk selected appropriate underwear. Then Becky tried on a pair of sandals, made of strips of soft, woven leather. She went into a back room to change into her new outfit.

"You look nice and fresh," he remarked when she came out and twirled around to show off for his approval.

"You'll want these." The middle-aged woman handed Zane the bundle of Becky's old clothes tied up with cord. He started to refuse, but then decided instead of throwing them away, manufactured cloth in this time and place might be useful, or worth something. If the clothes were beyond washing and mending, they could be cut up for rags if nothing else.

The general merchandise store held an amazing variety of items, and, for the benefit of the clerk, Zane said to Becky, "Didn't your daddy say to buy a poncho or two as well?"

"Oh, that's right," Becky said, picking up on his cue. "And he wanted three blankets, too."

The sales clerk looked over her reading glasses at them. "Are you folks heading upriver for the gold rush, too?"

"Oh, yes. My father is bustin' his seams to reach California," Becky said. "My mother is not eager to go. She's heard tales about wild Indians and such out on the plains."

"We have lots of folks in here stocking up for the long trip," the clerk said.

"Are there many boats heading for St. Joe?" Zane asked.

"The wharf is constantly jammed with them," the saleslady said. "And more coming up from St. Louis all the time. I think our goods here are a little cheaper than in the city, so a lot of the Argonauts are stocking up here before they leave."

"How long does it normally take to reach St. Joseph?" Zane asked.

"Oh, roughly a week, they tell me. It mostly depends on how much the weather or sandbars delay them."

"Sandbars?"

"Of course. Boats have to grasshopper over them all the time. But this time of year, there's still a good bit of water in the Missouri — spring runoff from the Rocky Mountains, you know. But, all and all, the muddy Missouri is still the river the oldtimers say is too thick to drink and too thin to plow." She smiled at the old joke as if she'd originated it.

While Becky wandered off to look at other things, Zane continued his conversation with the saleslady. The more he could find out in casual conversation, the better he could function in this new environment. "Is St. Joseph the jumping-off point for the wagon trains heading west?"

"That and Independence, a bit south of there," she replied, pointing to a wall map behind her. "My lands, I never saw so many folks lustin' after all those riches. Some who can't sell their businesses, up and slap a 'Closed' sign on them and leave anyway. Do you think there's really so much gold there that folks is picking up nuggets off the ground, like they say?"

"I don't reckon that's the case," Zane grinned. He stepped closer to the wall map and studied it. He was used to seeing maps of the United States with familiar state lines and settled boundaries. But this was entirely different. A large, irregular section of the middle of the country extended west and north from Missouri. In block letters it was marked, *INDIAN TERRITORY.* So that's what the boys were talking about. It appeared to cover much of what became Nebraska, and part of Kansas, Oklahoma, and South Dakota.

He turned away and noticed Becky gesturing at something on the far side of the room where the guns and harnesses were racked.

He wandered toward her and saw her pointing at tins of gunpowder and lead balls on display with Colt revolvers. Zane purchased a small leather pouch of .31 balls and several circular boxes of copper caps and a three-pound tin of gunpowder, thinking as he did so that his mother's ancestors had invented gunpowder centuries before. They very likely hadn't done mankind any great favors by their discovery. But, if the Chinese hadn't, someone else would have.

Zane wished he could find another pair of

sneakers, but knew there was no such thing here and now. His canvas and rubber shoes had been almost constantly wet, and the skin of his feet was white and wrinkled as a result. So he bought himself a pair of leather shoes that seemed to fit, but didn't feel near as good as his padded tennis shoes. A pair of woolen socks would be enough padding.

Jim apparently had no need of shoes in summer. He'd walked barefoot for so long, the bottoms of his feet were mostly horny calluses, apparently as thick as the soles of Indian moccasins, Zane thought.

He glanced around the store, trying to think of what else they might need, if they were to camp out, away from the prying eyes of people for a few days.

Zane and Becky returned to the yawl near suppertime loaded down with sacks of supplies. They'd decided to buy bacon and dried beans and flour, a few fresh tomatoes and some okra, a frying pan and cooking pot, stick matches — lucifers as people here called them — utensils and knives. In short, Zane and Becky had fortified themselves with everything they'd need to subsist on for a short time. But he missed the modern conveniences like paper napkins and plastic plates and cups — things he took for granted in his other world.

193

"Lawdy, I's mighty glad to see you two!" Jim said when they hove into sight. He took one of the canteens and turned it up, drinking more than a quart before pausing for breath. "Ah was dry!" he gasped, capping the canteen and putting it into the boat.

"We bought lots of stuff," Zane said, dropping the canvas sacks on the ground. "If I forgot anything, we can go back tomorrow."

"T'morrow be de Sabbath," Jim said.

"That's right. I'd lost track of the days. Stores won't be open." This was a time when commerce still observed the Sunday respite.

"We keep de Sabbath and onliest rest tomorrow," Jim said.

"We can go up to town Monday and scout around," Zane said. "But it's not likely we'll be meetin' up with those kidnappers," he added for Becky's benefit. He was afraid she'd be disappointed if no trace of them turned up after she was so wild about chasing them. The chances were very slim. This was a job for professionals.

As they sliced bacon and soaked some beans to cook over a driftwood fire, Zane filled Jim in on what the clerk had said, and the number of steamboats he'd seen at the wharf. "Lots of freight stacked everywhere, and people milling around like ants," he

194

said. "Most o' the boats are headed up-stream." He paused and thought for a moment. "Isn't it a little late to be starting out?" He recalled the histories he'd read of the pioneers traversing the snowy Rockies in the fall, and some even being caught by fatal storms, like the Donner party.

Jim nodded. "Iffen ah was goin', I'd start in de spring soon's dere's 'nuff grass for de animals. Dat be a long way across." He poked up the fire and placed a few flat rocks in a circle around the flames. "Gener'ly, dey be mo' storms in de spring wid hail and such, but ah reckon ah could put up wid dat. Dem mountains would be de tough part."

Becky was energetic, but quiet. She took over the cooking, making flapjacks from the flour. Zane was impressed. She might have looked like a spoiled rich kid who was an only child without a mother, but somebody — maybe the cook, Elsa — had taught her a few skills. And Becky was all for using them.

While the bacon was sizzling, Jim cleaned out his pistol and reloaded with dry powder.

Becky seemed very pleased with her new outfit, especially the sandals and the divided riding skirt.

Jim had selected a campsite that was far

195

enough back under the trees as to be out of easy eyeshot of anyone on the river, or walking along the shoreline. Over time, floodwaters had deposited a thick layer of sand fifty or sixty yards inland from the present river channel. It was level, hard sand with only a few scrubby bushes penetrating it.

"Now dat we's got blankets, maybe it be better if Miss Becky sleep in de boat, offen de groun', and away from de bugs," Jim said. "When me and Huck was on de river last year, we slept mostly in de daytimes. Don't seem to be as many critters walking 'round den."

Zane figured Jim was including snakes and wild boars in that assessment, but didn't say so to keep from scaring Becky.

After supper, when the tin plates, frying pan, and cooking pot were scoured out with clean white sand and rinsed in canteen water, the trio lounged about the fire, Jim smoking some fresh, aromatic tobacco.

Zane, who would've required at least an air mattress or foam pad to camp out in his father's zippered nylon tent at home, realized he hadn't given a thought to sleeping on the sand with only a blanket. Except for three nights in Sid Sawyer's bed, he'd spent the rest of the past week out of doors.

He began to plan ahead and assess their

options. If they saw no trace of the kidnappers, how could they tell Sheriff Stiles or the St. Louis police where to start looking? Becky could inform them about the house in the swamp where she was held. Yet, by the time any lawmen could locate that, the kidnappers and hostages would surely have vanished.

Becky would have to return home soon, in spite of the fact that Tom and Huck were still missing. At least the judge must be notified as to her whereabouts and her safety. But how to find the judge? He and Sheriff Stiles were possibly in St. Louis at this moment, thinking Becky was still a captive and wondering when Tom and Huck would show up in the yawl, according to the general plan. And of course, Zane thought, now the judge and sheriff would be thinking he and Jim were also missing. The law would be looking for all of them.

Maybe it would be best if he and Jim sold the yawl and the three of them returned to St. Petersburg by steamboat to tell their story to the authorities and let the law take it from there.

He and Jim and Becky had done about all they could for now.

CHAPTER 16

Tom and Huck lived the next several hours in terror of having their nostrils notched.

While the sun was setting, Smealey entered the room and set a small can of water on the floor. Standing in front of the boys, he began to strop his shiny Bowie knife on his leather belt. Grinning, Injun Joe's former partner tested it carefully with his thumb, then continued to strop the blade. He produced a small cube of lye soap from a pocket, lathered up his whiskers, and began to shave.

Tom tried to look away and think of something else, but still couldn't shut out the oily laugh and the *scrape ... scrape ...* sound of the deadly blade. Chills crawled up his sweaty back when he envisioned the keen edge coming for them next. He swallowed hard and looked across at Huck who was staring at the Bowie knife as if it were a coiling rattler.

After an agonizing several minutes, Smealey finished shaving, and wiped the blade on his pants leg. He tossed the remainder of the can of water onto the floor, laughed, shoved the knife back into its sheath, and walked out of the room.

Only then did Tom let out a deep sigh, realizing that, for the moment, they were safe from being sliced up. His heart rate began to slow down.

"Hucky, you think maybe we could slip out the back door after dark and snatch one o' them horses?"

"Even if they was tame enough, we'd need a rope or a halter, or sumpin'. And they're likely hobbled."

"Maybe we could grab the mane and sling a leg over the back of one of 'em," Tom said, trying to keep the desperation out of his voice.

Huck was silent for a moment. "Even if we could do it without them catching us, where would we go?"

"Anywheres away from here."

"We'd still be in a fix with no food or water, out in the swamp in the dark with our hands shackled. B'sides, if they catch us tryin' to escape, Smealey might notch our noses for sure."

199

"We can't stay here and wait for them to kill us."

"You said yourself Smealey ain't gonna kill us 'til they's over into the territory. We'd best wait for a better chance."

Tom acknowledged this was a wise plan, but could hardly contain the itch for action. Anything was better than waiting and wondering.

The sun dropped below the surrounding trees and long, gray shadows crept through the vacant rooms of the old house.

Tom leaned his head into the corner and dozed. When he opened his eyes again it was full dark. He could see light from a coal oil lamp leaking around the edges of the warped door to the next room. Sounds of Weir and Smealey moving about and the mumble of their voices. He listened. Not idle conversation. They were busy doing something in there. Maybe preparing to leave. He hoped so.

He started to speculate aloud about this, but the sound of Huck's steady breathing told him his friend was asleep. Best to let him rest, he decided, so he lay down on his back and willed his muscles to release their tension. They were safe enough for now. If he could only convince his fearful instincts of that he could relax and sleep.

■ ■ ■ ■

Tom awoke stiff and sore at dawn the next morning. His clothes were damp from dew he noticed when he wiped a sleeve across his face. The coolness of night was already giving way to muggy warmth. He sat up and saw Huck was awake. "What day is this?" he asked.

"Dunno."

"I think maybe it's Sunday," Tom said. "If I was home, I'd be washing up for church and Sunday school." He paused and thought about that. "I'd be figurin' some way to git out of goin'. But right now, that sufferin' don't seem half bad." He contemplated the relative pain of the two situations. "If a couple o' angels come and put them two to sleep and slid off our shackles like the time they rescued John the Baptist from prison, I'd be ever so grateful. I'd never complain about Sunday school again." The promise seemed hollow. "Maybe we should say a prayer for our delivery — ya know, since it *is* Sunday and all," he added so as not to seem to be calling on the Almighty only in time of desperation.

"I can't recollect a prayer," Huck said.

"We can make up one. How about, Lord,

give us some help." But then he thought that sounded too demanding. "Or at least don't help those two out there," he added.

"I reckon that's a good one," Huck said.

Tom was satisfied as well. "I guess now the onliest thing we can do is trust in Providence to . . ."

He was interrupted when Smealey entered the room and handed each of them two small strips of some kind of smoked meat.

Tom gnawed on it hungrily.

Saying nothing, Smealey dipped a gourd-ful of water from the small bucket he carried. He handed a drink to each of the boys in turn.

Then he left the room.

Tom finished the dried meat and almost immediately began to feel better.

A few minutes later, Gus Weir entered, holding a Colt pistol, and Tom's stomach dropped.

"Stand up. We're moving out."

The boys struggled clumsily to their feet.

Tom took another look at the man. He seemed to have changed. Then he saw Weir was wearing a false beard, glued on to match his black mustache. He had also altered the shape of his nose. Tom had seen enough amateur theatrical productions to recognize a putty nose. This one was considerably wider than the original.

The two horses were saddled and a canvas sack of gold coins was stuffed into one large pocket of each saddlebag while the other sides were filled with the small ham and other food items, utensils, and Weir's makeup for various disguises.

Huck was mounted on one horse and Weir took the reins and led the animal. Smealey rode the other horse and Tom was directed to take the reins and lead the horse, following along behind the others.

"Don't make no sudden moves," Smealey said. "I have my gun in my hand."

They started out through the tall weeds toward the far side of the clearing. There was no road or even a wagon track.

An hour later, they halted for ten minutes and everyone rested while the horses drank from a swampy pond and the humans drank from canteens. Then the riders and walkers switched places; Tom rode and Huck walked. At first Tom thought this a curious arrangement, but then realized if both he and Huck were astride at the same time, they might make a break for it.

Tom noted they were moving south. This way he knew would eventually take them to the Missouri River. He occupied his mind trying to figure out how far it was. But this quickly grew to be a tiresome and futile exercise.

So he switched and began to think of Becky. It warmed him to picture her as safe, though scuffed and bedraggled from her several-day ordeal. He wondered if she had had the gumption to take the yawl by herself and row down the river. Surely, she had seen the chance and taken his shouted advice. Being rather small and not hardened to physical labor, handling a boat of that size alone would have been a daunting chore. And she likely had to wait out the storm first. Even he and Huck would not have attempted it in the blackness and violence of that thunderstorm.

Keeping his mind occupied as they slogged along through thick forest and over patches of swampy ground, Tom whiled away the next several hours. Alternately riding and walking, he mentally escaped and the time went by much faster.

Sunset found them in a thinning stand of timber and in sight of a settlement some distance ahead. None of them had had anything to eat since morning, but Tom was more thirsty than hungry.

"That'd be St. Charles," Weir said as they halted the horses. "Scout around for a good dry spot to camp and we'll start a fire and cook some grub." He dismounted. "I'll fix you up with a white wig and some green glasses before we hit town in the morning."

The days in mid-June were long and it was only dusk when Smealey and Weir finished cooking the meal over the campfire. They shared a good bit of it with Tom and Huck.

Smealey unsaddled the horses and hobbled them on a nearby patch of grass to graze and roll.

Tom guessed his stomach had shrunk, but he ate until he was full — mostly food from their own yawl, he noted.

"We'll use up most of this food tonight," Weir told Smealey. "Maybe save a little for tomorrow, in case. We won't be needin' it after that. And we don't want to be totin' anything extra."

He spoke in front of the boys, who were eating with their hands still shackled. The iron bracelets were chaffing Tom's wrists raw, but he said nothing, sometimes pulling one sleeve and then the other down far enough to stuff under the metal rings.

"What's the plan from here?" Smealey asked.

Weir motioned for him to move away from the fire into the nearby woods, out of earshot.

Their low conversation didn't carry to Tom, who continued to fork up the ham and beans, apparently paying no attention to his captors. But he was all ears. To no avail, it turned out. The men were cautious and whatever plans they were making, the boys would know soon enough.

Two hours later, the fire was dying down, the horses were on a picket line strung between two trees, and Smealey was standing first watch. Weir lay under a blanket, his head on one of the saddles.

Smealey didn't look happy about performing sentry duty after a long day of traveling, but made no complaint. It was obvious to Tom who the boss was here.

Fatigued and pleasantly stuffed with decent food, he prepared to stretch out on the grass with an old quilt.

CHAPTER 17

By Monday morning, Becky, Jim, and Zane were rested and thoroughly bored with sitting around their camp near the boat. Although Zane said he still thought it a bad idea for a black man, a white blond girl, and a part-Chinese boy to be seen together in town, Jim was adamant that he should accompany them.

"I be yo slave, if anybody axe," Jim said.

Zane laughed. "I pretended to be Becky's servant the other day," he said. "Seemed to work okay." Both he and Jim had lost their hats in the storm, and needed some kind of head covering. Becky also wanted a wide-brimmed stylish straw hat she'd noticed in the mercantile.

To keep anyone from stealing the yawl, Jim suggested they hide both pairs of oars in the underbrush in the woods. They stowed their camp gear under a tangle of fallen tree limbs in the same area, taking only the canteens with them. Jim made sure the widow's Baby Dragoon was loaded, capped, and in his side pocket in case of trouble, or an extreme emergency. They planned to be as unobtrusive as possible.

After buying their hats, Zane asked the clerk directions to the sheriff's office.

"I don't know about the county sheriff," the young man told them, "but the police station is down that street two blocks and turn right. About a block north."

"What we gonna tell 'em, Zane?" Jim seemed nervous about facing the uniformed lawmen.

"We'll say what happened, and see if they can send word to the St. Louis police or Judge Thatcher or Sheriff Stiles." He was feeling frustrated that there was no telephone system with wires, or, better yet, cell phones with towers or satellites.

Zane led them in the front door, trying to look businesslike and confident. "We need to tell someone about a kidnapping," Zane said to the desk sergeant drawing himself up to his full five foot, five inches.

"Oh, do you, now?" He looked Zane up and down. The sergeant had a young face, but was completely bald except for a fringe around the ears. Bushy dark eyebrows gave him a look of authority. "I'll fetch the captain."

The three were ushered into another room where a middle-aged policeman, looking uncomfortably warm in a trim blue uniform, motioned them to chairs around a table.

"I'm Captain Shawnfield. What's this about a kidnapping?"

Zane told the story from the beginning, being as brief as possible. Then Becky added what she knew about the kidnappers and what they looked like.

The captain called in a clerk to take notes, then continued. "I've heard of Judge Thatcher. So you're his daughter?"

"Yes, sir." Becky, in her new clothes, sat with her broad-brimmed Panama hat on her lap, managing to look like a proper young lady in spite of her sunburned, mosquito-bitten face and arms.

"Hmm . . . So you were freed and two other hostages taken? Are these men demanding more ransom for the two boys?"

"No, sir. At least I don't think so." She continued to relate what she'd overheard about Smealey's desire for revenge.

The captain had read about the boys finding the treasure two years before. "I was relieved to hear about Injun Joe's death," he remarked. "He caused no end of trouble up and down the river."

Shawnfield questioned her closely about the looks and mannerisms of the two men, and what else she might have overheard of their plans.

"The one who's a slave hunter is named Gus Weir, and the other man was called Chigger Smealey."

The clerk was taking rapid notes.

"Can you send a telegraph message to the St. Louis police and ask them to notify Judge Thatcher?" Zane asked. "He thinks Becky is still a prisoner."

"I'd like to, son," the captain said, rubbing his freshly shaved chin. "There's a telegraph hookup between Washington City and St. Louis, but no telegraph here yet. I'll have to send word down on a steamboat. I'd advise you to go yourselves but there's a terrible outbreak of cholera in St. Louis right now. It's taken several thousand people in that city in the past few months, and is even now spreading upriver and out onto the overland trails toward California."

Zane groaned inwardly, glancing at Jim, who was sitting silently nearby. The black man showed no expression, as if he'd been used to hearing bad news all his life.

Zane didn't rightly know what cholera

was, since he'd never heard it spoken of in his time, but didn't want to show his ignorance by asking. If it was killing people at that rate, it must be bad.

"I'll have all the men I can spare on the lookout for these two men and the two boys," Captain Shawnfield said. "It's a long shot they'll turn up here, knowing the law is after them. But you never know. In normal times, we could do a pretty thorough job of scouring this city, but these aren't normal times. You may have noticed there are several thousand more people here now than we can easily accommodate. Everybody mad for gold and crowding aboard every boat that'll float to head upriver."

"We understand," Zane said.

"I'd advise you three to go on back to St. Petersburg, and we'll spread the word about these kidnappers. The abandoned house you mentioned is the old Wellsley plantation a few miles north in a bend of the river. I'll send a couple men up there to see if they can pick up a trail. If they were hiding out there, I feel sure they're not there now; they could have left by boat with no trail."

"They had two horses," Becky pointed out. "They wouldn't leave them behind."

The captain rose and opened the door for them. "If you like, I can have one of my men

211

give you directions to the steamboat ticket office. You shouldn't have any trouble booking passage the other way."

"We'll find it, captain," Zane said. "Thank you for your time and help."

The three of them departed.

"Well, *that* was a waste of time," Becky sniffed when they were walking back toward the waterfront. "Patting us on the head like nice doggies and telling us to go home."

"Well, you could hardly expect any more from them," Zane said, both irritated at her and frustrated at finding themselves at a dead end.

They ambled back into the downtown area, their spirits sagging.

Jim walked a few paces behind the two young people, head down befitting his role as a slave.

The streets were crowded with pedestrians, everyone seemingly in a hurry. Many were carrying grips or traveling bags, some trundling trunks on two-wheeled carts. Wagons of merchandise were loading and unloading at warehouses near the river. Commerce seemed to be booming. Even this early in the day, saloons were open and doing a good business.

Zane paused two blocks from the river and stepped back out of the way of the crush of pedestrians who were clumping along the boardwalk.

"Well, what do you want to do?" he asked Becky, including Jim in the question. "Shall we sell the yawl and go home?"

Becky frowned, staring off distractedly at the bustling crowds on the streets.

Zane saw her blue eyes suddenly focus on something and follow it along the street. As he turned to see what she was looking at, she brushed past him and darted out into the dusty street, dodging a buggy whose driver had to pull up his horse, cussing. Becky dashed up to a horseman, grabbed the bridle of his mount, and shouted, "Where'd you get this horse?"

The girl has gone crazy, Zane thought. The pressure's made her mind snap.

Watching for an opening in the passing traffic, he nimbly bounded out to her.

"What're you doing? Leave that man alone!" He grabbed her arm. "Sorry, mister," he said to the startled rider who was trying to regain control of his plunging animal.

"I know this horse!" Becky hissed in Zane's ear. "Smealey rode it."

"What?" Zane looked at the animal.

"See that white blaze on its forehead?"

Zane looked. He recalled the judge men-

213

tioning it when describing the abduction.

"I had plenty of time to notice little details while they had me," she said in a hoarse whisper. "A lopsided diamond. This is the one."

"Is this your horse?" Zane asked the bearded rider. "My girlfriend has an eye for good horseflesh. She's excited by beautiful animals like this."

Becky still had a grip on the bridle, and the rider was calming his startled mount, who was still fiddle-footing.

"What're you kids doing, anyway?" He sounded a little more than irritated. "This horse? Sure it's mine. Just bought him down at the livery."

"What livery? Where?" Becky demanded.

"We want one like him," Zane added, trying to give some reason for her impulsive action.

"It's called Horton's Feed and Livery down at the end of this street — about three blocks west."

"Thanks a lot, mister. Sorry for the inconvenience." Zane pulled Becky away and they skipped past a lumbering beer wagon to the safety of the boardwalk. Glaring at them, the rider moved on.

"Did you hear that?" Zane asked Jim, who was watching them from the shade of a doorway awning.

"Soun's like we best axe at de livery," Jim said.

Becky wanted to run all the way, but Zane restrained her. "We don't want to attract any attention," he told her. "Walk fast. We'll make it there soon enough."

They still arrived somewhat out of breath, and Zane sought out the proprietor, a fat man in overalls who ambled up, chewing on a broom straw.

Becky took a deep breath and asked the man if he remembered selling a horse today and described the sorrel with the triangular white blaze on its forehead.

"Sure do. A gelding. Sound animal, but I think he's been worked hard the past few days. I hardly had time to rub him down and feed him before this gent comes in and wants a horse, quick. He couldn't buy a boat ticket and decided he was gonna start off for Californy to . . ."

"Never mind the man who bought him," Zane interrupted. "Who did you buy him *from*?"

"Well, I bought two horses this morning, that sorrel bein' one. Two men and two boys came in here . . ."

"See! What'd I tell you?" Becky jabbed Zane in the ribs.

"Be quiet!" Zane turned back to the livery owner. "Can you tell me their names or what they looked like?"

The fat man frowned. "These animals ain't stole, are they? Maybe that's why I didn't have to pay much for 'em. They showed me a bill o' sale that looked genuine."

"As far as we know they're not stolen," Zane said. "We're only interested in who sold them and what they looked like."

"Wal, one had a full beard, black hair, and long nose. The other, as I recollect, wore green glasses and had long white hair."

"Did you notice the boys?"

"Nooo . . . They was about your age, I'd guess, kinda lean and sunburnt, hair hadn't seen no comb or scissors for a spell."

"Did the boys say anything to you? Did they speak at all?"

"Don't recollect them saying nothin'. I took advantage of the low asking price for those animals, paid the two men, and they hightailed it like they was in a hurry."

"What time was that?" Zane asked.

"Hmm . . . Early. Maybe four hours ago. Not long after sunup." He looked at them with curiosity. "These folks friends o' yourn?"

"Yeah," Zane said quickly before Becky

could reply. "We was supposed to meet 'em here in St. Charles and take off upriver for the gold fields, but I'm afraid they might have taken a boat ahead of us."

"What names did they give you?" Becky asked.

"Let me think . . . The one with the full beard — his name was Ordway. I believe the other one called himself Phillips. Or, maybe 'twas the other way 'round. Not sure. I thought you knew them."

"These men have a checkered past and sometimes operate under different names. No sense makin' themselves too available to the local law, if you know what I mean," Zane lied quickly. He was becoming more adept at this. "They ain't good friends of ours — only someone we plan to travel with — share expenses, you know."

"If they give you a bill of sale, was there a name on it?" Zane asked.

"Yeah, they gimme a paper." He led the way into a cubby at the end of a row of stalls and fumbled around in a cigar box on the homemade desk.

"Here . . . Now that's curious . . ." he remarked, glancing at the document as he held it out for Becky and Zane to see. "When these horses was bought, the name of the buyer was Gus Weir. Well, I can't be

217

responsible for any o' that shiftin' of identities and false names. I'm an honest businessman . . ."

Before he finished speaking, the three were out the door.

CHAPTER 18

As soon as they were twenty yards from the stable, Zane huddled with the other two. "They've been here and sold the horses, so wherever they went, they have about a four-hour head start on us."

"I *knew* there was a good reason we shouldn't go home yet," Becky said, barely able to contain her excitement.

"Any ideas, Jim?"

"Iffen dat be me, I be fo' gettin' far away from heah."

"They sold the horses, and they didn't rent or buy a buggy or wagon, which they could've done right there," Zane reasoned. "So they have to be travelin' by river. It's easier and quicker than any other way," he stated, mentally eliminating nonexistent trains.

"Dey be stagecoaches runnin' heah and dare," Jim said. "Dat be de onliest other way to go, I reckon."

"Yes, I'd forgotten about coach travel." In boom times like this, did stagecoach lines even keep a record of passenger names?

"I have a feeling they didn't go by coach," Zane said. "Four of them crowding into a coach with other passengers, it'd be nearly impossible to keep Tom and Huck from giving away the game for any length of time, unless they were asleep or out cold — maybe knocked out with chloroform. Then how could the men explain that to other travelers if they were carrying two unconscious boys? No. It has to be the river." He turned to Jim. "If you were those men, dragging Tom and Huck along as prisoners, which way would you go if you were traveling by steamboat?"

"Up de river," he said without hesitation.

"Why?"

"De sickness be downriver at St. Looie, and de police dere gots de telegraph. Most folks after de gold out west, so I do my best to blend in wid de crowd headin' fo' St. Joe."

"You wouldn't take a boat back north toward Iowa?"

"Why do dat? Folks all 'round St. Petersburg gots to know 'bout de kidnappin', so dey be on de lookout."

"I heard Weir say he would go to New

Orleans when this was all over," Becky said. "He had sort of a drawly talk, like folks I've heard who come up from Loosiana."

"Well, according to the description that liveryman gave us, they're in disguise — except for the boys, of course."

"Yes," Becky said. "Neither of the men had a beard when I was with them. Weir had a black mustache and a thin nose. Smealey, the other one, sort of wavy reddish brown hair — not white."

"Okay, so how do we check all these upbound steamboats?" Zane wondered aloud. He felt keenly his inexperience in this alien world. At least here, there were no security checks and officials were a lot more lax than in his modern world.

"Do you want to go after them?"

"Yes!" Becky almost shouted.

"Ah reckon ah gots to go if you two goes."

"Then it's settled. We'll buy tickets on an upbound boat. We'll have to leave the yawl. At least our camping stuff is hid pretty well until we return." He paused and thought. "If we can't find any trace of them at St. Joe, we'll notify whatever lawman we see there, and we'll have no choice but to go home."

"We'll worry about that when the time comes," Becky said, obviously thinking that time would never come.

"There's at least a dozen boats at the wharf right now," Zane said. "Let's see how many of them are upbound, and then ask for the two men under their real names — Weir and Smealey — and the fake ones — Ordway and Phillips — even though they might be using different names by now. And we'll ask the pursers for two men who fit those disguises and see if they went aboard with two boys."

Zane paused and took a long drink from one of the canteens they still carried on straps over their shoulders. The other two also decided they were thirsty, too.

"Okay, let's start at the lower end. If you notice a boat preparing to cast off, run to it first. I don't know any other way to do it. I'm sure there are a lot of lost strangers in a town that's funneling all these gold rushers through, so nobody will question why we're looking for these people."

While they were talking, they'd been walking quickly toward the levee.

"Becky, to cover these quickly, you take the first and third boats, and I'll take the second and fourth and so on. They won't give the time o' day to Jim because everyone will assume he's a slave, but I have a job for him while we're doing this." He

222

pulled a small spiral notebook from his pocket and tore a page from it. "Jim, take this note back and leave it in the yawl where it won't blow out, but someone can find it." He addressed the note to Judge Thatcher and Sheriff Reuben Stiles. He wrote that he and Jim and Becky were safe, but were in hot pursuit of the two kidnappers, Gus Weir and Chigger Smealey, who had the gold and were holding Tom and Huck as hostages. They were upbound on a steamboat for St. Joe. He told whoever found the note to send help as fast as possible. He dated and signed it, then folded it once and wrote URGENT on the outside in large letters. "This is written in ballpoint pen so it won't smear if it should get rained on," he said, handing Jim the note. "If you see anything in our camp we'll need, bring it, because we might not get back there again."

Jim nodded and took off at a trot.

Becky was already at the head of the gangway of the first boat, talking to the lean purser with jug-handle ears. The young man was all smiles and apparent cooperation.

Zane grinned. *Most likely the best-looking girl who's paid him any mind in a long time.* He sprinted for the second boat in line.

They alternated boats, sometimes having to wait a couple of minutes to accost the purser. Over a half hour later, Zane hit pay dirt at the eighth packet, the *Penrose*.

"Yeah, two men and two boys like you describe came aboard," the purser said. "We were scheduled to cast off this morning with a full passenger list and a loaded cargo hold, but the engineer is ashore now trying to find a replacement for a faulty pressure valve. The other two valves are working all right, so we've kept up some steam. But we likely won't get away until at least four this afternoon. We might even have to lay up overnight."

"Can you tell me what names they used?"

"False names?" The young purser arched his eyebrows and flipped back the pages of his log book. He ran a finger down the column. "Gus Ordway and John Phillips."

Zane nodded. "What about the two boys?"

"Sam and Archie — minors. No last names."

"This lady," he gestured at Becky who was coming up the gangplank, "and I and our slave, Jim, want to purchase one-way tickets to St. Joe."

"Half the country does," the purser said with a resigned air. "We're loaded to the gun'ls."

"We'll take deck passage," Zane said before he thought.

"If we'd taken on all the requests for deck passage we've had today, there wouldn't be room enough to stack the cordwood to run the steam engine."

"Any other boats you know of going upriver today?"

"Sure. Four or five, but I expect you'll hear the same story from them."

Zane nodded and then turned and escorted Becky back down the gangway to the wharf.

"What did he say? I didn't hear all of that," she said, looking her concern at him.

"They've taken passage on this boat. The bad news is, they have no room for us."

"Can't we take another one? They're all bound for St. Joe."

"The purser says they're likely all as full as this one."

Zane stood irresolute for a few moments, staring with unseeing eyes at the bustle of draymen and foot passengers around them.

"I'll try a bribe," he decided.

"What good will that do, if there's no room?"

"Sometimes gold will work wonders when it comes to finding space, or room in a hotel — things like that. I hate to do it because I think it's lowdown and underhanded and gives privilege to the wealthy. But . . . this *is*

Tom and Huck's money, and I'd be spending it to help them, so I don't reckon it's a bad thing to do."

He was hardly aware that his words and expressions were beginning to conform to those of the locals.

Zane looked back toward the boat where the purser was busy chalking a sign in large letters on a piece of wood next to his station at the head of the gangway. It read — FULL.

"Looks like he means it," Becky said.

"Worth a try, anyway," Zane said. "Now that we have these men almost in sight, I don't want to try another boat and take a chance on letting them escape."

"When is the *Penrose* leaving?"

"Late this afternoon or in the morning, he said. They busted a pressure valve and have to find another one."

"Then why not go to the police station and report to Captain Shawnfield? Let him send someone to arrest them and free the boys."

Zane chewed his lip, weighing his options. "Good idea. You stay here and wait for Jim. Keep an eye on the boat to make sure those kidnappers don't get off. The police station is about a mile from here, but I should have plenty of time." He started away, then

226

paused. "Oh, here. I meant to give you this earlier." He fumbled under his shirt for the money belt, and plucked out two ten-dollar and two-five dollar gold pieces. "Hide these somewhere. Never know what's gonna happen and I don't want you to be without money if we should somehow be separated."

"We won't," she said, closing her hand over the coins. "Hurry!"

Zane took off at a fast walk. He felt lighter than he had in several days. A great weight had been lifted from him. He and his new friends had accomplished what they set out to do and the kidnappers would not escape. Tom and Huck would be rescued and the gold would be recovered. He and Becky and Jim would be heroes.

But he'd better stay out of the publicity or risk being called crazy if anyone found out he claimed to be from a future century. Did Providence have anything to do with all this? He pondered the inscrutable. When he'd first arrived last week, he would have dismissed the existence of Divine Providence. But now . . . certain happenings that could not be explained except by chance or Providence — like Becky recognizing the blaze-faced horse on the street. That coincidence had led to the discovery of the criminals they sought.

He decided to leave philosophical questions for another time as he quickened his pace, weaving through heavy pedestrian and wagon traffic on the street.

"Zane!"

He stopped and looked around at the milling crowd. Had someone shouted his name or was he hearing things? Nothing. He started again at a fast walk.

"Zane! Wait! Zane!"

He was sure of it this time. A familiar deep voice. He turned and saw Jim laboring toward him at a run, dodging horsemen, shouldering aside pedestrians, then ignoring their glares.

"Mars Zane," Jim panted coming up and stopping, hands on knees. "Come quick! De boat . . . de *Penrose* . . . she be leavin'!"

"What?" A chill went up his back.

"Yassah . . . Miss Becky say come fetch you . . . jus dis minute dey be haulin' up de gangway."

Zane was still three-quarters of a mile from the police station. Too far.

Jim stood up, wiping his sweaty face with a sleeve. "She say dey hold de boat a few minutes if you hurry."

"We can't board the *Penrose*. There's no room."

"Miss Becky, she done bribe de purser.

Dey gots one room if you come quick."

"Let's go!"

They turned and sprinted toward the waterfront.

They turned and sprinted toward the waterfront.

CHAPTER 19

Frustration, panic, desperation — all these
feelings flashed through Zane as he outran
the winded Jim to the waterfront.

He saw Becky gesturing to him and he
put on an extra burst of speed. She turned
and waved at the deckhands who were
hanging on to the ropes that had levered up
the gangway. They lowered it back down to
the dock.

Jim came laboring up, hat in hand, sweat
pouring off his glistening face.

They staggered up the ramp after Becky,
and the trio gathered on the main deck.

Mooring lines were being cast off and up
came the gangway again.

Zane was seeing spots before his eyes from
his maximum exertion in the hot sun. He'd
never felt this bad after a soccer game, so
why now? Maybe the muggy, windless air.
He labored to fill and expel air from his
lungs as he leaned over, sweat dripping from

his nose. He should be accustomed to having no air-conditioning by now. He looked up at Becky, who seemed as cool and fresh as ever.

Jim was used to hard work, but he, too, was laboring for breath. *Maybe I'm not as wimpy as I first thought.* He leaned against a stanchion and looked to Becky for direction. "Where to?"

She pointed. "This way," and led them toward the forward stairs.

The boat trembled and began to move.

On the second level, they went to the aft end of the boiler deck along the catwalk. She unlocked the last cabin door on the larboard side and they entered.

Zane could hardly wait to find out how she'd accomplished this, but details could wait until they were all safely ensconced.

The room was small, but neat. Fresh white paint on the walls brightened the space. It was furnished with the usual washstand, water pitcher, basin, and one chair.

"My! Dis be fust rate," Jim commented.

Zane agreed. He flopped down on the lower bunk. "Okay, tell me how you managed it," he said to Becky, who looked like a cat with feathers in her whiskers.

"As you said, it's astounding what gold can do." She smiled. "It cost that whole $30 you handed me awhile ago. Besides," she added smugly, "it sometimes helps to be a girl."

And a pretty, flirtatious one, at that, Zane thought.

"My hat's off to you!" He saluted her by removing his new straw hat and tossing it down beside him.

Jim had taken the chair and his breathing was steadying down.

"The purser — name of Farley Nicholson, by the way — told me the captain of this boat always reserves one small stateroom for visiting dignitaries, so he won't be caught short, especially if one of the directors of the line shows up. The crew is supposed to keep mum about this cabin, but Farley, er . . . Mister Nicholson said since there were no bigwigs aboard this trip, he could take my $30 in gold, in addition to our regular fares, of course, and then he'd split the gold with the captain. He was sure the captain wouldn't mind the extra cash. Mister Nicholson will come 'round directly to collect the money for our tickets."

"Did you tell Farley how old you are?" Zane asked.

"Not exactly."

"He's a grown man in his twenties."

"Well, I might have let it slip that I was

almost sixteen."

"In about two more years, maybe." Zane shook his head. "You did great work finding this cabin. Just be careful about leading him on," he warned.

Jim offered no comment.

"I thought Farley said the boat wouldn't leave until late today or in the morning," Zane said.

"Right after I started talking to Mister Nicholson, one of the crewmen came up and told him the valve had been replaced. The engineer borrowed an extra one from a nearby boat, and we'd be casting off right away."

"Well, here we are." Zane stood up, stretching his leg muscles, which were beginning to stiffen from the hard sprint. "Maybe we shouldn't have wished so hard to make it aboard with these kidnappers. Woulda been a sight better if I'd reached the police in time to come arrest these two." He thought of a quote he'd read somewhere, *Of all sad words of tongue and pen, the saddest are these: It might have been.* "With a telegraph or telephone, Captain Shawnfield might've called ahead to have the law arrest these men upriver somewhere." He sighed. "But we don't have none o' them modern marvels," he finished, falling into the local

233

vernacular again.

"Dat be Providence dippin' an oar in," Jim said with a resigned air.

"Maybe so," Zane said. "But it ain't Providence that's faced with dealing with these two; it's us. We have to come up with a plan. First off, we must make sure Becky stays in this cabin so Weir and Smealey don't somehow have a peek at her, because she's the only one of us they've seen before."

"You mean I have to stay cooped up in this little cabin in the heat?" she groaned. "Once we're sure they *are* aboard, why not go to the captain and have them arrested and chained up until we reach a town with a sheriff?" Becky suggested.

"No. Let's lie low and keep mum for a while first," Zane said. "We'll scout around and figure out where their cabin is located. I'd guess they have the boys hid away somewhere."

"Best not tell de captain," Jim said.

Zane agreed. Adult white authority was not to be trusted, and Jim knew this better than most. "If we go to the captain, and he questions Weir and Smealey, they could claim to be Ordway and Phillips and completely innocent," Zane said, playing devil's advocate. "Even if we found Tom and Huck and they swear they're hostages, where's the

234

proof? Our word against theirs. Becky could testify against them, too, but this boat is not a court of law. The captain would likely say we can prefer charges against them at the next town, but he ain't likely to chain 'em up on our say-so. As they say where I come from, we would have blown our cover. Our identity would be known, and we'd be at their mercy. We might disappear overboard some dark night with knives in our backs."

Becky gave a slight shudder at this. "And to think men would do such things for gold."

"I reckon most people are subject to 'gold fever,' " Zane said.

"It be like horses eatin' loco weed," Jim added. "Sho to make 'em crazy."

"Becky, you've done more than anyone to put us on the trail of these criminals. Tom would be proud of your skills as a detective," Zane said. "If you'll agree to stay in the cabin for a while until we can take a look around, I'll be grateful and will fetch your meals to you," he added, hoping to placate her. "Maybe after dark, whether the boat is running or tied up, you can put on your wide straw hat and we can walk around outside without being recognized."

"Oh, all right, if it'll help rescue the boys."

"Great. Thanks a lot."

"Ah put de note in de yawl, like you axe," Jim said.

"Good. After that boat sets there for a time, I'd bet somebody will try to steal it or at least find out who owns it. It has the name of the *Millicent* on it, so they'd likely think it was stolen or lost overside. If they try to take it, they'll have to furnish their own oars, since we hid our two pair," Zane said. "If they find the note, they might be curious enough to take it to the police." But Zane knew the chances of anything positive coming from that were only slightly better than securing help from a message in a bottle.

"I think we've done all we can for now," Zane said, thinking back over their actions. "Jim, let's rest here a few minutes and then go out and have a stroll around." He glanced at the inside door of the cabin. "Were does that lead to?"

"Into the main saloon," Becky said.

"Saloon? Like an old west saloon?"

"No, silly. It's only another name for the main cabin of the boat. This packet is a small stern-wheeler, so it's not a big room, but it's where the meals are served and they have dances and such. There's usually a bar up forward where passengers can buy drinks." She glanced at him. "Don't you know how most steamboats are made?"

"No. We don't have steamboats where I come from."

"Where's that?"

"Well, it's a long story. Tom and Huck know all about it. When we rescue them, we'll all sit down together and I'll explain it as best I can. It's pretty complicated," he said. "But meanwhile, can you tell me how this boat is arranged?"

"Sure. Once you start exploring, it'll help to know what you're looking at," Becky said. "And Jim can help, too. These little passenger cabins are called staterooms because they're sometimes named after states of the union — mostly on bigger boats. These rooms are arranged along both sides of the second deck, called the boiler deck. Each room, like this one, has two doors. One opens outside to the walkway where we came in, and the other opens into the main saloon." She sat down on the lower bunk beside him.

"The main deck below us is where the boiler and steam engines are that drive the paddle wheel. It's also where the cordwood is stacked. The hold carries cargo, and any overflow is stacked on the main deck. Cheaper tickets are for deck passage, and people sleep there, too. You can see it's pretty crowded with the crewmen trying to walk around all that clutter and do their work of firing the boiler and tending the capstans and such."

She smiled and continued in the voice of a schoolteacher. "The top deck, above us, is called the hurricane deck, I guess 'cause it's mostly open to the weather. This boat's too small to have a Texas, but that would be a few rooms all clumped together up there. This clump of rooms would be quarters for the captain, pilots, and crew. On this boat, though, rooms for the crew are in other places. Of course, the pilothouse stands up top, above everything. Now, does that help?"

"It surely does. Thanks." He saw she was back in good spirits.

Zane stood and stretched. "Jim, you want to take a stroll around?"

Jim put on his hat.

There was a sharp knock on the outside door.

Zane's heart skipped a beat, and they glanced at each other.

"Who is it?" Becky asked.

"The purser, ma'am, to collect for your tickets."

Zane let out a deep breath. He hadn't realized how keyed up he was.

Becky turned the door latch and opened

it. Farley Nicholson stepped in, glancing curiously at Jim. "Since you didn't purchase tickets ashore, I'll take the fare now."

He gave her the price and Zane paid it from several gold coins he had in his pocket without exposing the money belt. It was a dollar too much for three one-way tickets to St. Joe. "Keep the change," Zane said. "And please ask the steward to send up a small mattress we can put on the floor."

"Right away." The purser didn't address him as "sir" apparently due to the fact that Zane was a good ten years younger. Nicholson nodded and backed out, with a last appraising glance at Becky.

Before the door closed, Zane noticed the cabin was number one.

Becky had mentioned earlier the cabins were numbered from aft forward, odd numbers to larboard, even to starboard.

They waited a couple of minutes before Zane and Jim left. "Keep the door locked," Zane cautioned Becky as they departed.

The heat in the sun was fearsome and Zane was glad to have his hat. In his previous life, he'd rarely worn a hat, except for a baseball cap sometimes.

"Jim, let's go down and start on the main deck and work up," Zane suggested.

They reached the forward stairs and Zane

had to keep turning around to talk to his friend. "What are you doing back there?"

"Anybody lookin', ah walks behind, so's ah 'pears to be yo slave," Jim said in a low voice.

Apparently, long, hard experience had honed this man's survival instinct.

"Jim, where I come from my dad told me some of his white friends say all black folks look alike."

"Dat mebbe so, but dis man, Weir, he be a slave hunter. He *knows* black faces. He study 'em fo' his bisness."

"You're right."

Farley Nicholson had told Zane the truth about one thing — the *Penrose* was loaded about as full as she could be with cargo and people. There was less than three feet of freeboard between the main deck and the water, Zane noticed as they stepped carefully among the boxes and bales and lounging passengers.

St. Charles had disappeared behind them and the shoreline along this broad stretch of river was nothing but solid forest. The water was high and the brown muddy current was sweeping along logs and planks, limbs of trees and bushes — even an occasional outhouse.

When Zane passed near the firebox, he

240

felt a withering blast of heat from an open door. How could these crewmen stand to work down near this constant heat? He noted about half the deckhands were black. Surely there weren't that many free men around here. If slaves, then who owned them? He assumed an armed guard was posted while the crew was wooding up at remote woodyards. But it still seemed very possible one or two determined slaves could slip away to freedom in the twilight of an Illinois forest. Slaves were expensive, and even more expensive to have recaptured.

A few of the rougher-looking men eyed him, possibly resenting the fact that a part-Chinese boy could own his own slave. Maybe his rich parents had favored him with an upriver cruise to escape the outbreak of cholera in St. Louis. And they'd sent along a slave to wait on him. In Zane's imagination, at least, this is what lay behind some of the baleful stares.

He was glad when they went topside to the boiler deck again and strolled past the outside cabin doors on both sides. One or two of them stood open for the slight breeze created by the boat's forward motion.

Most of the passengers, it seemed, were outside moving about the decks, lounging under the overhangs, dressed in light dresses and shirtsleeves, thirsting for a breeze.

Zane and Jim went into the main "saloon" as Becky had called it. It was carpeted and contained several small tables and chairs. A few of the men at the forward end were playing cards and smoking cigars. Lunch was over and it was too early for supper.

A coffee urn stood next to a bar stocked with various wines and hard liquors.

Zane took two coffee cups out of a rack and filled them for himself and Jim, handing one to his friend as they went out the forward end of the main saloon and up to the hurricane deck.

A slightly cooler movement of air caressed the wide expanse of water, and at least a dozen people were strolling the deck to take advantage of it. A foamy wake was being kicked out behind the boat as they churned up against the current in the middle of the engorged stream.

The top half of the pilothouse was visible through the glass front window as Zane and Jim walked by. The spokes of the large wheel were in continuous motion as the pilot made smooth corrections to their course, apparently dodging floating obstacles and driftwood.

They paused in the shade of one of the twin smokestacks to sip on their coffee and take in the scene.

"Take it all 'round, dis travelin' by steamboat sho beats rowin' a skiff."

"Is it even better than a raft?" Zane asked.

"Ah don't know 'bout dat. Dis be mo' fun; a raf' be home."

A wise man many think of as ignorant, Zane thought.

Zane suddenly felt Jim's fingers grip his arm above the elbow. He saw the man's eyes focused on something over Zane's shoulder.

"Don't tun aroun'," Jim said in a hoarse whisper. "Ah see two men. Dey fits de size and look o' de kidnappers."

CHAPTER 20

Zane casually shifted his position to one side of the smokestack and flicked a glance in the general direction. When he saw they weren't looking his way, he focused on them. Some twenty feet away, two men were facing each other and talking.

The slightly taller one wore a full beard and had a wide nose that might have been altered. The other was clean-shaven, and white hair protruded from under the brim of his hat.

He'd verify this later, but he had a feeling these were the two they sought. He'd seen no other passengers who came even close to the description Becky had given them. Instead of a mix of older and younger passengers, this boat carried a preponderance of young males, obviously headed for the gold fields. These two didn't fit that group. They looked somewhat older.

"Jim, can you keep an eye on those two

until I come back? I want Becky to see them."

"Dey best not see *her,*" Jim said.

"I have a plan to prevent that."

"Ah keeps 'em in sight, Mars Zane."

Zane slid down the forward companionway and back to their cabin. He rapped on the door. "Becky, it's Zane!" he whispered, his mouth close to the crack of the door.

A few seconds later the door opened and he slipped inside. He almost tripped on the matting on the floor the steward had apparently delivered to serve as their third bed.

"Let's fix up a signal, since we only have one key," she said.

"Okay. How about two raps, a pause, and one rap?"

"Good. Tell Jim, too."

"I think we've spotted the two kidnappers up on the hurricane deck. Jim's watching them, but I want you to see them."

"They'll know me," she said.

"No. I'll ask the steward to give me some mosquito netting and make a veil for you that will fit over your wide hat. It'll hide your face and hair. Then you can come on deck with me. If they see you it won't matter. They don't know me, and they won't be expecting you on this boat anyway. Besides, you have on different clothes than the dress

245

they last saw you in."

"Okay."

"I'll be back in a few minutes. Remember our signal. And shove that mat under the bunk."

He was out the door before she could reply.

Twenty minutes later, Zane and Becky found Jim lounging near the entrance to the main cabin, in low conversation with one of the black waiters. When he saw them he gave a slight nod in the direction of a table several feet away where the two suspects sat.

Zane maneuvered Becky casually to another table and seated her where she had a good view of the two men. "I'll fetch some coffee," he said, and moved away. He glanced back at her and realized the mosquito netting was a good disguise; it formed a tent over her wide straw hat and was tied under her chin, completely obscuring her face and blond hair.

He returned to the table with two mugs of black coffee, even though he knew she couldn't drink it without lifting the veil.

They feigned conversation for a few minutes. The men under surveillance did not even glance their way.

246

"Okay, I've seen enough," she said quietly. "It's them."

She rose from the table and Zane walked with her slowly out on deck. A minute later Jim came up and stood beside them. They all leaned on the rail, as if watching the timbered shoreline slide by.

Zane, touching her arm, could feel her tremble slightly. "I had a good look at both of them. Even with that disguise I'd know Weir anywhere. When I saw those eyes — it was like looking into the eyes of a snake. Fake nose, fake beard — they don't matter. I'll always see those eyes in my nightmares."

"Did you hear their voices?"

"No. Didn't need to."

"Jim, can you keep watch on them and find out their room number? I'll walk Becky back to our cabin."

"Ah sholy will."

"When you come to the cabin, knock twice, pause, and then once, and we'll let you in."

Nearly an hour later, Jim rapped on the door with the signal and the three of them sat down, ignoring the afternoon heat to plan their next move.

"Dey be in number two cabin," Jim reported. "Mostly straight across de saloon from us on de stabbard side."

"Next thing we need to find out is where they're keeping Tom and Huck," Zane said.

"It'll be suppertime in a couple hours," Becky said after a minute of silence. "You know they won't let Tom and Huck come out and eat in the main cabin. And they won't let the steward carry any food to them, either. Weir or Smealey will take the boys' supper to them, wherever they are. All we have to do is watch where they go."

"Simple plans are best," Zane agreed. He smiled. "I reckon Tom would throw more style into it with a few complications, but he's not planning this operation."

They discussed how they'd affect a rescue once they discovered where the boys were being kept. But here their plow struck a stump.

After a minute of silence, Becky suggested, "Maybe I should describe to the captain what these two kidnappers look like — tell him they're wearing disguises, and now have the boys hid on board somewhere. If we don't discover where Tom and Huck are, the captain could have the boat searched."

Zane looked at Jim, then replied, "I'm new here, but I'm guessing it'll take more than the word of two kids and an ex-slave to convince a steamboat captain to confront two of his passengers with an accusation like that."

"We needs de proof," Jim said.

"Let's take one thing at a time and wait and see," Zane said. "Something will suggest itself."

"De ways o' Providence be mighty strange," Jim added. "But it point de way by 'n' by."

Their plan worked. While Zane ate in the main cabin, Jim, in his role as servant/slave, took Becky's supper to her, along with a bowl of stew for himself.

Meanwhile, Zane lingered at his table until Weir and Smealey were finished, then mingled with the milling passengers outside and followed Smealey. He unlocked cabin number six on the starboard side and entered with the tray of food. When he came out a minute later, he was carrying what one of Zane's great grandmothers used to call a "thunder mug" — a chamber pot. Holding it carefully, Smealey headed toward the boxy privy mounted far aft.

That made sense, Zane thought. The boys would not even be allowed outside to use the bathroom. And Smealey, being the underling in this kidnapping operation, would have to accept the most onerous chores.

Zane, feeling elated, reported to Jim and Becky that the boys were apparently being held prisoner in the second cabin from that of Weir and Smealey — number six.

"Maybe they couldn't reserve adjacent rooms," Zane said. "The boat is full so there's likely somebody occupying the room in between."

"We'll have to pick the lock some dark night," Becky said. "But I don't know how to pick a lock. If we try to force our way into the room from the inside door that opens into the main cabin, somebody will see us."

"I don't know anything about locks or how to open them, either," Zane said, "except with a key. Maybe you could charm Farley into lending you the key."

"No . . ." Becky was very reluctant. "He might want something in return. Besides, I'm not sure the purser has keys to the rooms."

"Mebbe we bust de door," Jim said.

"That would make a lot of noise and get us in all kinds of trouble, especially if the boys aren't in there," Becky said.

"I'd stake my life they're in number six," Zane said.

"If we bust 'em out, we could do it when de boat tie up fo' de night," Jim said. "Den we kin jump fo' de shore and steal away in de woods."

"Boats that don't run at night usually tie up at woodyards where there are men who sell the cordwood," Becky said. "Even if we slipped past them, where are we gonna go — lost in some strange forest at night?"

"Why not wait 'til we reach St. Joe, and then bust 'em out if it don't look like the kidnappers are getting off the boat there with Tom and Huck?" Zane suggested. "There'd be lots of people around forming up wagon trains and such and we could find help right quick."

"Dat be a good idea," Jim said. "Let a few days slide along. How long do it take to get dere?"

"I'll ask the pilot," Zane said. "There are a few other things I need to ask him about this boat anyway. If we decide to bust the door down, I reckon you're strong enough to do it," Zane said to Jim.

The black man nodded. "But it be mighty noisy wid all dat wood crackin' and split-tin'. Zane, you's mighty handy wid an axe. You could slip out one of dem axes down on deck near de woodpile."

"That's right. Two or three whacks in the

right place and I could have that latch chopped right outa there. Better than bustin' the whole door."

"I guess the main thing is not to rush and do something rash, and mess up the whole rescue," Becky said.

"Okay, we'll sleep on it and give it some more consideration. Give Providence a chance to work," he added.

The next day, Zane and Jim accosted the pilot when he came off duty at noon and engaged him in casual conversation as he went below to his midday meal.

"Name's Billy Randall," the middle-aged, graying man said, thrusting out his hand. "Come join me for lunch while we talk."

Zane introduced himself, then introduced Jim as a free man. Randall and Zane sat down in the main cabin while Jim, for appearance's sake, stood by, pretending to wait on them. Randall wiped his flushed face with a bandanna and drank a tall glass of water to cool off.

"Your job looks as hard as chopping firewood," Zane remarked.

"Yeah, I'd say that was a good comparison," Randall replied. "You fellas from Missouri?"

"St. Petersburg," Jim replied. "Mo' den a

252

hunert miles up from St. Looie."

"Yeah, I know that village. So you fellas are more familiar with the Mississippi? That's a mighty different river from the Missouri." He took a sip of coffee and turned to Jim. "You ever hear of a Missouri River pilot by the name of Jacques Desire?"

"Nossah."

"He's a negro from Louisiana, and everyone calls him 'Black Dave.' Don't recall if he was born free or set free, but he's been on the river for a number of years, and just a crackerjack pilot. Thought you might know of him. He and I worked on the same boat about five years back. One time we was on the Upper Missouri past Council Bluffs. About a dozen Santee Sioux got riled up about something, and started shooting at our boat from the shore. I was at the wheel, and Dave was beside me when the bullets commenced to fly past our heads and shattered the glass in the pilothouse. Well, Black Dave, as calm as you please, stepped outside and behind one of the smokestacks until the shooting stopped. I said, 'Dave, those Injuns are mighty poor shots. You afraid of stopping a slug?' He stepped back into the pilothouse and said, 'No, but if I did, my troubles would be over. My eyes are my only means of making a living and I must protect

253

them from flying glass.' "

"Dat be a mighty smart man," Jim allowed.

"Time for lunch," Randall said, pushing back his chair.

"You sit dere. I bring de food," Jim said. He went to a side table and ladled out dipperfuls of steaming beef stew with potatoes, onions, and carrots, and brought two bowls to the table with chunks of bread.

To avert any mutterings and stares from the other diners, Jim did not eat, but sat alone on a bench by the wall, several feet away, where he could still overhear the conversation.

As they ate, washing down the meal with coffee, Zane asked, "How long does it take to reach St. Joe?"

"Depends. Three or four days is excellent time. Mostly, due to sandbars, it takes upward of a week or so."

"Is that running day and night?"

"Mostly days."

"How come the boat didn't stop last night?"

"The *Penrose* is a well-built boat, and fairly new. But we didn't stop because the river is full to overflowing with water right now. It's the spring melt in the Rocky Mountains flowing down this far that causes it." He wiped up some gravy with a piece of bread and popped it into his mouth. "And there's another reason. I bet you can't guess what it is . . ."

"What's that?"

"One way this river is different from the Mississippi is that it carries a greater load of silt. And on bright, moonlit nights like last night, the moon reflects off water that is pale, muddy-brown, and full of silt. On my eight-to-twelve watch last night, it was easy to see and steer and avoid a few sawyers. In addition, we're bulling up against the current, staying in the channel as best we can because we can ride right overtop those nasty sandbars. It's shoal water and sandbars that drive pilots crazy. We'll have enough o' that later this summer."

"So we likely won't be laying up overnight if the weather stays clear?" Zane asked.

"That's right. I'm hoping for a fast run to St. Joe. I'm mighty sick of being delayed for hours and days by having to grasshopper over bars. On the upper river it's even worse. But these flat-bottom boats are designed to draw no more than a foot or two of water when empty. I once heard a pilot brag he could run a Missouri River packet on nothing more than a heavy dew. And another fella, to top that, said, he could

255

spill a keg o' beer over the side and run four miles on the suds." He chuckled. "Although why anyone would want to waste beer like that, I don't know."

"Billy Randall!"

The pilot looked up, then rose and thrust out his hand. "By God, Andre Carrick! I didn't know you were aboard. Come, join us."

The pilot made the introductions and the newcomer pulled up a chair. He was a shade under six feet tall, Zane guessed, lean and handsome, bold features, weathered by the sun. His black hair was tinged with gray. Zane had a hard time estimating ages of adults, but put this man at a well-used fifty. He was clean-shaven and wore doeskin britches and a white cotton shirt.

"Fellas, Andre is an old friend of mine — a French Canadian. Once upon a time he worked for the American Fur Company."

"Yeah, we had a falling out and all that's behind me," Carrick said, easily. "I been guiding wagon trains for a few years now."

"How's business since the gold rush started?" Randall asked.

"How do you think? I could have a dozen jobs at a time if I could somehow multiply myself. Why don't you quit this everlasting puddle-jumping and come join me? There's good money in it. Something new every day."

Randall chuckled. "To each his own, my friend. The river can be aggravating for sure, but when I'm off duty, I can fall asleep in a soft bunk and know when I wake up my hair will still be attached."

"Touché."

Zane was all eyes and ears. This man was a genuine wagon train guide? He'd read about such men, barely realizing they had existed. They were like the gods of old — legendary and barely credible. And here was one of them sitting at his table.

"What're you doing on this boat if you're so busy?"

"Had to go down to St. Louis to straighten out some orders for supplies and have 'em shipped up to St. Joe. Most of these Argonauts are not your steady, practical farmers of years ago. This new bunch heard the word 'gold,' threw down everything, and started west without a thought as to what they were facing or what to bring. My job is to take whatever money they have and see to it they are supplied with the basics in food and transportation, then do my best to herd 'em across the continent alive."

They chatted a bit longer while Randall and Zane finished their meal.

"We'll visit some more before we debark," Carrick said, rising. "Gents, it was good to make your acquaintance." He shook hands with Zane, nodded to Jim, and went out on deck.

"That man has more lives than a cat," Randall said when the scout departed. "If he ever opens up and starts tellin' stories around a campfire some evening, he could entertain you for hours with tales that would make your hair stand on end. Even yours," he chuckled, pointing at Jim's curly mat.

This was the type of tasteless joke Zane would never have heard in his previous world.

But, nevertheless, he was impressed with this frontiersman. He figured Carrick could be called upon for help in any crisis. Zane was glad this man was aboard the *Penrose*.

CHAPTER 21

Zane and Jim went back to their cabin after lunch, taking a bowl of stew and a chunk of bread for Becky. Zane didn't want to leave her alone for hours on end cooped up in the hot cabin with no company.

"What did you two find out this morning?" she asked, digging into her food.

Zane told of talking to the pilot and meeting Andre Carrick.

"I'm sorry Tom wasn't there. He would've said this guide was the ideal one to join up with and go adventuring amongst the Injuns," Zane remarked. "This man has already been there — many times."

"So, what's our next move?" she asked.

"Well, if the weather stays clear, we won't have to tie up overnight, the pilot says, so we'll likely reach St. Joe in another three or four days," Zane replied. "And the river's high enough where we might not go aground on any sandbars and have to use

259

the derricks to grasshopper over them." He sounded as if he knew what he was talking about. Ten days ago he'd never heard of any such thing. "I'm thinking that St. Joe would be a good place to make our move to rescue the boys."

"What if those kidnappers get off in St. Joe and take the boys with them instead of staying on the boat to go upriver?" she asked.

Zane pondered this. "Is there any way you could persuade Farley to see if their tickets are for Council Bluffs or Yankton or some place farther north?"

Becky shook her head. "I'm taking your advice and staying away from Mister Nicholson."

"Well, no matter. We can play it by ear, and see how things develop. What do you think, Jim?"

Jim looked solemn. "Dis be de dangersome part o' de plan. If we bust in an' snatch de boys de night befo' we hit St. Joe, we could hide 'em in here fo' a bit."

"That's if we're not caught in the act," Zane said. "Why don't we watch Weir and Smealey for a couple of days and see if there is a routine they follow every day and every night. It'd be best to go for Tom and Huck late at night when everybody's asleep except

260

maybe the pilot and engineer and a couple deckhands down below. Nobody near the passenger cabins, anyway."

Jim nodded his agreement.

"Then, if we break 'em loose without anyone seeing, we can do like Jim says, and hustle them over here to hide until we dock."

"We be stirrin' up de hornets, fo' sure," Jim said.

"Well, they don't know we're aboard, so maybe I can jimmy the lock so it looks like Tom and Huck busted it from the inside," Zane said. "If the boys can't be found, maybe the kidnappers will think they jumped overboard to escape and drowned. In any case, I'm guessing they'll figure the hostages have served their purpose and be glad they're gone. Then they'll grab the ransom and light out into the territory."

Zane wished he had asked Captain Shawnfield if United States law applied in Indian Territory. He made a mental note to ask the next lawman he saw, but in the meantime, he voiced his question to Becky.

"I don't rightly know," she said with a frown. "I'll have to ask my father. But I'd think not. I've heard tales of outlaws and all kinds of rapscallions fleeing into the territory to take refuge. But, then, maybe the law applies there, but they're able to hide out without being seen because it's a wilderness." Then she returned to the matter at hand. "If you break the door latch, will it be on the outside door to the catwalk, or the inside door that opens into the main saloon?"

"I'm thinking the outside door would be safer. One or two of the crew on duty, or a passenger with insomnia, might be wandering through the saloon, looking for a snack or coffee or something in the night. It would only take one person to ruin the whole plan," Zane said. "Jim, make sure your pistol is in good working order."

Jim patted the side pocket of the light coat that he wore, regardless of the weather. "Ah gots it right heah. When ah went back to de camp, ah fetched along mo' powder, shot, and caps."

"Good man," Zane said. "Let's hope we don't have to use a gun, but I'm glad we have it for protection — if needed."

Zane thought of all the men he'd seen on board carrying belt guns, including Weir and Smealey. Apparently, it was normal practice for men in this day and time. He couldn't help but contrast this with the electronic security in his own day against carrying weapons aboard airliners. But then, maybe no terrorists were in the habit of blowing up steamboats, which apparently blew up often enough on their own.

"I'll wait a couple days and then ask the pilot again when he thinks we'll dock in St. Joe," Zane said, thinking out loud. "Then I'll write a note and slip it under their door to let Tom and Huck know we're fixin' to bust them out and what night to be expectin' it. Don't want to catch them unawares and scare the daylights out of them."

"Dat be right smart," Jim agreed. "Iffen you bust in widout no notice, dey likely take and lam you over de head wid a chair."

For the next two and a half days, Jim and Zane were all eyes and ears. Nothing the kidnappers did escaped their notice. They observed the habits and routine of Weir and Smealey — when they came out of their cabin in the morning, when they retired at night after cards, brandy and cigars in the main saloon, when they strolled around the decks, the fact they were never seen apart and didn't talk to any of the crew. Jim and Zane took care not to be seen conferring too often on deck or in the main saloon.

Bucking the current required a good head of steam, and the fireboxes were consuming cordwood at a fast rate. The boat stopped at woodyards twice each day, and Zane considered their chances of rescuing the boys and making it safely ashore while the boat was tied up for a short spell. Tempted though he was, it was always daylight and the wilderness surrounding the river looked daunting. They'd stick to the original plan. And it was not only the rescue they had to think about; they also must devise a plan to catch the kidnappers and recover the gold — a tall order.

Jim and Zane compared notes in their own cabin, sharing the information with Becky, who seemed to be catching cabin fever. "I can't sleep *all* the time while you two are away," she said. "I am so hot in here and I need a bath."

Zane told her to be patient, that her exile would last only a couple more days. Zane took her out to walk around the deck for some exercise and fresh air after dark when she wasn't obliged to wear her concealing mosquito net over her hat, and to use the privy at the stern of the boat. He filled the pitcher with fresh water every day to allow her to wash her face and hands, and brought her meals. Even though she was close to his own age, and very independent, he felt as protective of Becky as of his own little sister, Miranda.

264

■ ■ ■ ■

Their luck with the river didn't last. On Friday morning, Zane and Jim were standing on the hurricane deck aft of the pilothouse when they were suddenly pitched forward to the deck as the boat ran aground.

Pots and pans crashed in the galley below. An outburst of yelling and cussing erupted from crew and passengers. Orders were shouted, and the paddle wheel slowed to a stop.

Billy Randall descended from the pilothouse and ran forward to get a better view of the bow.

Then he came back and bounded up the steps again. "Couldn't have been avoided," he said to Zane as he passed. He didn't seem upset. "Submerged sandbar right in mid-channel. Come on up and watch."

Zane needed no second invitation. He sprang up the steps and stood well out of the way, looking through the glass windows at the brown current swirling past the boat. Deckhands forward on both larboard and starboard were busy probing the depth of the muddy water with long poles.

"The boat's not hard aground," Randall said, standing to one side of the wooden

265

wheel, his left hand on a spoke. He opened a speaking tub to his right and ordered the engineer to reverse engines.

"With the amount of water in the river right now, we should be able to back off." He uncapped the speaking tube again. "Hard astern!"

Zane could hear the paddle wheel thrashing.

"Even though we're heavily loaded, this'll drag 'er off by main force, or will drive enough water up under the hull to wash away the sand and refloat her." He stood sideways, looking forward, then aft. "You can never tell about this river," he said. "Judging from the current on the surface, any layman would guess it's at least fifty feet deep here. But I tell you one thing, I'll take two dozen groundings over one snag. A snag will rip the bottom out of 'er in a heartbeat."

After two or three minutes, Zane felt the boat shudder and then move and a cheer went up from the deckhands below as the *Penrose* floated free.

Randall gave the order for half speed ahead and then began to feel his way forward, concentrating on his work, apparently forgetting Zane was still there.

Several minutes later, the pilot seemed to

266

relax again. "If we can avoid hitting any more of those, we'll be in St. Joe in the morning."

Zane's ears pricked up. "In the morning? Will you run tonight?"

"Don't see no reason not to," he replied. "Should be another clear night with plenty of moonlight. We'll bypass Independence and Westport Landing. All our passengers are bound for St. Joe, the main jumping-off point for Oregon and California."

Zane thanked him and left the pilothouse. Jim had gone forward to watch the boat maneuver from the shade of the smoke-stacks.

"Meet you in the main saloon for coffee," Zane said as he went by down the companionway.

By the time Jim arrived, Zane had obtained a sheet of the boat's stationery from a wooden rack on a rear table in the main saloon.

He sat down with Jim in a corner, took out his rollerball pen, and, after some reflection, wrote the following in large, block letters so the boys could not misread it: WE WILL BUST IN AND FREE YOU LATE TONIGHT. LIE LOW AND KEEP MUM. ZANE, BECKY, AND JIM

He studied it for a few moments, then

decided he didn't need to add any more; that was sufficient.

He read it aloud to Jim. "I'll slip this under their door after supper. They might not have any lamplight to read it later on."

"You gwine t' use de axe?"

"Yeah. But I'll wait until after dark to borrow it off a rack by the woodpile so no deckhand sees me."

Zane sipped the coffee Jim had brought for him. His nerves were on edge. This was far beyond any experience he'd had in his previous life. And the stakes were high. This was no game.

CHAPTER 22

That afternoon, while Jim kept an eye on the kidnappers, Zane studied both doors to their own cabin, examining how the locks and knobs were made and installed. The exterior door was thicker and more weather-resistant. Both had panels of thin wood that a man or a strong boy could splinter with a couple of hard kicks. Why hadn't Tom and Huck done this and escaped before now? Either of them could squeeze through one of the lower panels if it were kicked out. Maybe they'd been drugged and were too weak to make the effort.

Zane squatted on his heels and worked the knob and the latch on the inner door of their cabin. The whole superstructure of this boat appeared to be made of relatively lightweight pine instead of some hard wood. "Becky, I'll need someone to hold a lamp for me tonight. I'm sure there's an overhead oil lamp in their cabin like the one in here,

269

but I can't take time to fool with it. Only need a light for a minute to see what I'm doing with that axe."

"I'll hold it."

"No. I don't want anyone to see your face. Besides, if something goes wrong, Jim can protect me." He thought for a moment, holding the inner door partially open and looking across the main saloon. "It's not over twelve or fourteen feet across this room. Maybe I should bust the inside door instead," he muttered to himself.

"What?"

"Nothing. Thinking out loud." Outside, any noise they made would be offset by the breeze, the swishing of the paddle wheel, the low thumping of the machinery and noise of the steam escape pipe. Inside, the axe blows would be confined and probably heard by someone. He wished a thunderstorm would come up and mask the chopping. But, if it were storming, the boat would be tied up, which would make no difference to the escape.

"How do you know Weir and Smealey won't find the note you slip under the door for Tom and Huck?" Becky asked.

"Jim and I been watching those two men for a few days now. Their routine never varies. They don't go near the boys' cabin after

270

they deliver their supper to them."

"I hope you're right. Whew! This is scary."

He stood up and shut the door. "I'm going below to check the axe. Lock the door behind me."

On the main deck he lounged around until the deckhands and passengers were otherwise engaged, then stepped up and used his thumb to gently test the edge of the axe, which rested in a rack on the bulkhead. The crew kept it razor sharp.

Now, he'd go find Jim and they'd snitch a loose lantern.

At suppertime, Zane watched as Smealey took the boys' food to them, entering through the inside door to their cabin. Then he came out and locked it. The same routine as before.

Later, during the long summer twilight while the boat continued to plow upstream, Jim took a nap on the mat while Zane tried to rest on the lower bunk. But sleep wouldn't come. He had to be fresh for tonight. After nearly an hour, he gave up and went outside to stroll the deck. When the sun was resting on the western tree line, he took his written note and slipped it under the door to Tom and Huck's room. No one was on the catwalk, so he knocked sharply four times on the door before walking away. He hoped they would be forewarned. If not, the escape would still happen.

"Zane! Zane!" A hand shook him out of a restless doze. "It be time." Jim was squatting beside his sleeping mat on the floor, holding a partially sheltered hurricane lantern.

Zane came instantly awake and glanced at his wristwatch. A few minutes until two a.m. Becky's eyes from the upper bunk looked large in the dim light.

Zane put on his sneakers and slipped out the door and down to the main deck. The boat was plowing smoothly along in the bright moonlight.

The passengers sprawled and curled up on the main deck were all asleep. Even the two deckhands on duty were sitting forward on the bitts, heads down and dozing.

Zane quietly eased up to the aft bulkhead that closed off the steam engines. He moved confidently as if he was supposed to be there. He was partially shielded by the stacks of cordwood and boxes and barrels of freight as he slipped the axe out. Holding it alongside his leg he ascended the aft stairway. Jim was waiting with the lantern shuttered. In a moment they were only dark shadows under the roof overhang beside the outside door of cabin six.

Jim eased open the shutter of the lantern to allow a sliver of light to escape, then stood back out of the way.

With a last look around, Zane hefted the axe and brought it down with force, splintering the upper panel. Three more hard whacks had the latch mechanism hanging from the damaged wood. More noise wouldn't matter now. One more blow and the knob and lock assembly fell out. They were quickly inside and Jim opened the lantern, kicking the ruined door shut behind him.

Huck and Tom were wide awake, shackled by their wrists to the bedposts.

"Here, hold your hands like this," Zane panted, stretching the short chain across the wood. He prayed his aim was good. The blade struck the links and sparks flew. Three hard whacks and the chain parted.

Huck held his hands the same way with the chain around the wooden bedpost. Two more quick, powerful blows with the heavy axe blade and the chain popped in two and slid over the splintered post.

Making a quick decision he pulled Jim forward to hold the light on the inside door latch. Four more hard blows smashed the wood and knocked loose the knob and lock so the door could be kicked open.

The dimly lit main saloon was empty and in three steps they were across the dozen feet to their own room where Becky held the door open for them. They shot inside and she closed and locked it.

Tom and Huck dove under the lower bunk, pulling their feet out of sight. Becky vaulted into the upper. Zane opened the outer door, looked right and left, and flung the axe into the river. Then he closed the door quietly, engaged the bolt, and he and Jim, breathing heavily, lay down on the mat and lower bunk as if they'd been there all night.

A minute or two later they heard some commotion and voices raised outside. Whoever had been on watch had heard the banging and crashing and come to investigate.

Zane's heart was pounding and he mentally practiced what he'd say if or when the mate came with questions.

He heard footsteps thudding on the catwalk, then voices inside the saloon. Would the boat's officers take the chance of aggravating all the other sleeping passengers by pounding on their doors at this time of night?

If the cabins were searched, the mate and

others would likely wait until daylight. Tom and Huck would be discovered and he and Jim and Becky would be in trouble. He'd have to tell the story to the captain.

What would the kidnappers say? Even when the officers realized that cabin six was occupied by two boys Weir and Smealey had brought aboard, the kidnappers would deny any knowledge of what'd happened.

Zane had never met the captain, so knew nothing about the man. If he tended to blame the black and the young people for the break-in and damage, Zane would ask to see Andre Carrick and explain the situation to him. The metal handcuffs hanging to the boys' wrists should be some proof their story was true.

Zane wondered what was happening outside, but forced himself to remain still for the few minutes it took for his breathing steady down.

Jim had left the hurricane lantern burning dimly on the floor in the corner. While there was still some stirring and voices in the main saloon, Jim rose and slowly cranked open the small transom above the inside door.

". . . nothing we can do about it until morning," the rough voice of the mate growled.

"Passenger list shows two boys in that room."

Zane didn't recognize the voice.

"Robbery you think?" the mate said.

Zane was straining to hear as the boat's officers moved away from the door.

"Could be. We got a rough bunch aboard."

"Knock up the men in number two. They brought 'em aboard."

"Tried, but they ain't in their room."

"That's almighty str . . ."

The voices faded as the men moved forward.

Zane caught his breath. The two kidnappers had fled. But where? They couldn't escape the boat in the middle of the river at night with two heavy bags of gold.

Becky was looking over the edge of the upper berth, and Tom and Huck had crawled out from under the lower. They gave and received quick hugs all around before hunkering down for a quick conference.

For once, Tom seemed at a loss for words, but tears glistened in his eyes in the lamplight. The two boys looked pale and drawn as if they'd just awakened from some long sickness. "We heard the knock and saw the note under the door," Huck said. "I stretched fur as I could and drug it over

276

with my foot. Me and Tom was able to read it. Then I shoved it in my pocket. Got it right here."

"Okay, now that we've sprung you, the kidnappers have bolted," Zane said.

"Should we go to the captain right now and tell our story?" Becky asked.

Everyone was quiet for a moment, trying to think what was best.

"Maybe if we tell him right now, they can arrest those two when they try to go ashore."

"Or, the captain will blame us for not coming to him right at first, instead of busting up that cabin." Zane looked at his watch. "Let's wait a few hours until we dock. Sometimes doing nothing is the best course."

Jim nodded his agreement.

"Is that agreeable to everyone?" Zane asked, looking around.

They all assented. "As my grandmother used to say, *'Don't shake hands with the devil until you meet him in the road.'* If we're bound for trouble, let it come to us, rather than rushing to meet it. Weir and Smealey must still be aboard. We can bide our time, and let them sweat. We'll be ready when the boat docks." Zane turned to Tom and Huck. "Let me see those wrists." The boys' wrists, still encircled by the metal cuffs that had chafed the skin, were raw and bleeding. The wounds had not been cleaned or treated.

"Ah'll snag some whisky fo' 'em," Jim said.

"No, let me go," Zane said. "You stand guard here." He eased open the inside door and went across the deserted saloon with only a quick glance in the direction of the opposite broken door.

He discovered all the bottles behind the bar were locked in a metal rack. He'd have to wait until later; he wasn't about to damage any more property.

It was after three o'clock.

CHAPTER 23

"That's the last of 'em," Captain Horace Smith said. "No more passengers debarking at St. Joe." He glanced at Zane who stood beside him at the head of the gangway. "If what you say is true, those two — Weir and Smealey or Ordway and Phillips — or whatever they call themselves, somehow slipped off the boat earlier. I've had my men search this boat bow to stern and even down into the cargo hold. There's no sign of them."

Zane's stomach sank like a leadsman's weight. "Okay, Captain. Thanks. I'll pay for the damage to the doors of that cabin."

"Never mind. The company has insurance and will take care of it. We have some damage every trip. I'm grateful those two boys are safe." Tom, Huck, Jim, and an unveiled Becky stood to one side.

"Good luck from here on." The white-haired Captain Smith shook hands with

Zane and nodded to the others as he turned to supervise the unloading of the cargo.

Tom, Huck, Becky, Jim, and Zane had no luggage to haul ashore, and had paid fare only one-way. If they decided to return, they'd have to buy tickets and wait for a downbound steamer.

They all trooped down the gangway. A hundred yards or so beyond the wharf was the edge of what looked like a massive, several-acre wagon sale or stockyards, or livery, or maybe the beginnings of the largest tent meeting in the history of Missouri. Wagons, horses, oxen, and people were milling about in what could best be likened to a huge ant hill. Wood smoke, cooking meat, moldy hay, the ammonia odor of urine from hundreds of animals, earthy smells of ground churned up with tons of manure — a repulsive miasma that was only made tolerable by a westerly breeze wafting across the river from Indian Territory.

Zane caught his breath. The sight and odors were almost more than he could bear. "What *is* this?" he asked aloud.

"Welcome to St. Joe, Missouri, lad," a voice said as a tall man swept past him from the boat.

"Mister Carrick!" Zane shouted impulsively.

The scout turned around. "You know me? . . . ah, yes, I met you a few days ago. But I forget your name."

Zane reintroduced himself. "Are all these people heading west?"

"That's right," Carrick said.

"Why are they here?"

"Only two ferries cross the river and they run on a first come, first served, cash basis when the water isn't too high. What you see here is all the backup." He swept his arm at the milling mob of humans, animals, and wagons churning and re-churning the half-dried mud.

"Looks like our work is laid out for us," Tom said.

"What work?" Zane asked.

"Why finding them kidnappin' robbers, of course."

"I thought we warn't gonna do that, once we was shut of 'em," Huck said.

"Mebbe best to let blame well alone," Jim added.

"They put us to no end of trouble and they stole our $12,000," Tom stated. "We gonna let them waltz off into Injun Territory with all that gold? All these folks out here waiting to cross the river are headin' west to dig gold outa the cricks and ground. Those two had it handed to them."

281

Zane could see his point when he put it like that. He glanced at Becky. What was she thinking? Her neutral expression indicated she was game for whatever the others decided.

"All you five together?" Carrick asked.

"Yes."

"And you're looking for those two men who stole your gold and held you hostage? I heard some folks talking about it on the boat."

"That's right." Tom held up his wrists with the metal bracelets still attached. "I don't know how they slipped off this boat before we landed, but they did. Maybe swum ashore hanging onto a couple logs o' cordwood."

Carrick looked off at the milling throng with campfires smoking here and there. "Maybe I can help you," he said. "I don't have to report to my wagon train until later today." He looked at Tom. "Meanwhile, I can direct you to a locksmith if you boys want to shed that jewelry."

"That would be most kind of you," Becky said.

"Come with me; I'll walk into town with you." Carrick hoisted his saddlebags over one shoulder.

About a mile away they came to the busi-

282

ness district and Carrick led them to a locksmith shop. The smith had the locks opened in a minute without asking any questions. He started to toss the shackles into a trash barrel.

"Wait," Tom said. "Give me one of those for a souvenir. Since I'll have scars on my wrists, I want to show what did it." He thrust one of the bracelets into his pocket.

Zane started to pay the smith, but Carrick waved him aside. "I'll take care of this. It's nothing."

As they walked back toward the crowded campsite of the gold rushers, the issue of what they would do was still undecided, Zane thought. If they didn't find any sign of the two kidnappers, they could either go on to California, or return to St. Petersburg and give up. Somehow, he couldn't see them doing this.

"Let me show you around," Carrick offered. "I have some time to kill. The party I'm guiding has twenty wagons and a few dozen animals — horses, oxen, and mules. I'll go by the camp and drop my saddlebags and then we'll see if we see hide or hair of your robbers. In my experience, there are a lot of wanted men who head west, and blend in with all the honest folks."

For the next two hours, Andre Carrick

283

walked around with them, visiting with other wagon trains, introducing himself, and casually asking about the two kidnappers, letting Becky, Tom, and Huck describe the pair.

Near three o'clock, the wagon master of a long train who was next in line for one of the ferries startled them all when he said, "Yeah, I seen two men like that just this morning."

All of them were at full attention instantly.

"You know where they went?"

"Naw. Never paid 'em no mind after we concluded our business," the white-bearded wagon master said.

"What business?" Carrick asked.

"They was in the market to buy two saddle horses. Normally we wouldn't have had any to spare, but one of our wagons dropped out. The wife took sick and the husband and kids decided to go back to Illinois. They had some extra stock they wanted to turn into cash so they sold the two horses. Good, strong mounts. These two men paid cash for horses and saddles."

"Did they have a couple of heavy saddlebags?" Zane asked.

"Hmmm . . . Matter of fact, they did. No other luggage. Guess all their gear was packed in 'em."

Tom and Huck's gold, Zane thought. From the looks on their faces, the others were thinking the same.

As they turned away, the wagon master added one afterthought, "They was in a rush to be off and said they was gonna bypass the ferry and swim their mounts over the Missouri. I warned them it was dangerous, but they only laughed."

Carrick moved away with his group. "Sounds like your kidnappers," he said. "I sure would like to help you catch them. I hate to think they're loose over in the territory where there ain't no law."

"You reckon they're already across and goin' like smoke on the trail to California?" Tom wondered aloud.

"Very likely, since they bought their horses several hours ago. If they was in a hurry, like the man said, they likely bought a few provisions and hightailed it," Carrick said. "I reckon about now they're either several miles out toward the Platte, or they're in the bottom of the Missouri," he stated, matter-of-factly.

People in this time treated life and death with equal indifference, Zane thought. You took your chances and either lived or died as a result. This environment would make a boy grow up quick. Given what he'd already been through since last week, he felt about twenty years old.

"I want to light out after them," Tom said.

"How do we manage that?" Becky asked.

"I don't know, but we can't let them off scot-free," Tom said. "I ain't hangin' my head back in St. Petersburg admittin' I failed and let two outlaws who treated us so mean run away with our gold besides."

Carrick faced them. "If you kids are dead set about trailing these two, you're welcome to join my wagon train. You don't want to travel by yourselves, even though there is one adult with you," he said, indicating Jim.

"Mister Carrick, is there some way I can notify my father, Judge Thatcher, that I'm safe?" Becky asked.

"Where is he?"

Becky looked at the boys.

"Me and Huck was supposed to row our yawl on down the river to meet up with the judge and the sheriff at the St. Louis levee," Tom said. "But that was more than a week ago. They likely give up on us by now. No telling where they might be."

"Can't send them a letter without an address, unless you mail it to St. Petersburg," Carrick said. "And mail delivery is mighty sketchy anyhow. No tellin' when, or if, they'd even receive a letter."

They all thought for a moment.

"Well, never mind," Becky said, with a sigh. "If we head out after those outlaws, somethin' bad might happen to me yet. So I don't want to send a message that I'm safe, and then have him later find out I'm dead or something." She shuddered and bit her lip. "Best we go on and see what happens. I'll contact him when this is all over."

"The wagon train can't travel fast and we might not see those outlaws at all," Carrick cautioned. "So don't boost up your hopes. You have any money for provisions?"

"Yeah, we have a little gold."

"How much?"

Zane looked at Jim. "I haven't counted it, but I think a little less than two hundred left." He would not have revealed this to anyone else, but felt Carrick could be trusted.

"Okay, that's plenty. If you want to go all the way to California, it might take all of that."

"Is that your decision, then?" Carrick looked at Becky, then Jim and Tom and Huck, and lastly at Zane who'd been talking.

"I'm agreeable," Huck said. "We don't have nothin' to lose."

"Only a little time and some money,"

Becky added.

"Po' niggers don't have no luck, but ah wants to catch dem robbers, too," Jim said.

"I go where they go," Zane said, wondering how he'd fare if he were in this alien world on his own.

"Okay," Carrick said. "You won't need a wagon since you're not carrying anything along. Supplies and animals are expensive here because of the demand. But I'll help you buy some horses and saddles and what little food and gear you'll need. If you don't go all the way to California, you'll have enough to return." He gestured. "Whoever has the money, come with me. We have to supply you quickly. Time is moving and my train is second in line to cross the ferry in the morning."

All of them went with Carrick to buy their mounts and slickers and food. The total they wound up having to spend put a larger dent in their remaining money than they'd expected.

Zane's main worry was riding a horse. He'd have to find a gentle animal since he had no experience.

CHAPTER 24

The train of twenty wagons with all their stock started across the Missouri next morning at 6:40 a.m., the ferrymen heaving on the hawsers that drew the flat raft across the turgid stream. It took four trips to land them all on the other side.

Zane had the feeling they were in a different country and he was relieved to be beyond the mass of people, wagons, and animals. The previous afternoon, after considerable searching, haggling, and eyeing of horseflesh by the experienced Carrick, a sturdy riding mule was selected for Jim, who seemed very satisfied with the choice since he had experience riding mules. The animal was a bit fractious at first, but Jim had a way with animals, Huck said, and Zane noted the black man stroking the mule's neck and talking quietly into one of the long ears. In no time at all Jim and his new mount were a team.

A small pinto was selected for Becky; Tom and Huck bought bays, and Zane was given a good-sized burro when he admitted to zero riding experience. He wanted no high-strung horse that would shy at a snake or would jump out from under him at the first crack of lightning. Burros were sure-footed and not as likely to break a leg on rough ground or in a prairie dog hole. "Besides," Tom said, "I druther sleep near a burro anytime since they'll stomp a snake in a minute. Them sharp hooves will keep you safe from copperheads for sure."

After looking at the muddy, swirling water, Zane had his doubts that Weir and Smealey had been able to swim their horses across with at least fifty pounds of gold coin. But they had disappeared from the *Penrose*, and how else but swimming with the gold — perhaps with the help of driftwood. These two appeared to be fearless. If they were on the trail ahead, would Zane and the others ever catch up?

The expedition quickly settled into a dull routine. Nobody traveled faster than the plodding oxen. But it gave Zane a chance to become used to his gray burro. Becky and Carrick had given Zane a few riding pointers and he soon settled in, although he could never become accustomed to the idea of a living animal under him who might rebel at his slightest lapse of attention and throw him. He would have much preferred an impersonal mechanical device like his familiar bicycle.

Would they have to travel all the way to the west coast? How far would Weir and Smealey go? They already had their golden treasure. No need to travel cross-country to the gold fields where they might have to work. He guessed they'd ride two or three days into Indian Territory and then hole up until they thought the law had quit looking for them before returning to the states. Then Weir would likely start south to New Orleans. Tom said Smealey had mentioned lighting out for Texas, which had recently been won from Mexico.

Ahead and behind Zane could see other wagon trains. He certainly hadn't expected anything akin to a crowded twenty-first-century highway, creeping as slowly as traffic on a torn-up interstate.

As they moved northwesterly into what later would be southeastern Nebraska, the terrain began to change. Trees thinned out, with copses in hollows apparently growing where water was abundant.

The sky grew wider, the land emptier. As long as the soil was still damp and no dust was being churned up, the five rode at the end of the train. As the mounts plodded along, the young people conversed until they ran out of topics or the afternoon sun hammered them into a semi-doze.

An hour before sundown, the train halted for the night. Tom and Huck rode out with a few other men from the train to find firewood.

Zane and Becky were too exhausted to stir after they unsaddled their mounts and Becky showed Zane how to rub down the animals and give them some oats to eat. Then one of the men from the last wagon in line showed him how to hobble his burro so he couldn't wander off.

"There have already been too many trains over this trail," Carrick explained when Becky wondered about the lack of grass for forage. "This prairie grass will never provide the needs of all the animals who pass over it in a season. We're already well into June and pretty soon, as we move farther west, the men will have to take the oxen and horses a long distance to either side of the trail to find sufficient grass. Trains can't carry enough hay or grain to feed them for the whole trip. When we hit the desert near the Humboldt River, we'll be down to feeding the stock a slurry of flour mixed with whatever water we can find."

The first night Zane found himself falling asleep over his beans and bacon as he sat on a blanket near the campfire. His watch said it was already 11:48 p.m. and it was barely dark. Then he realized his watch was still on Eastern Time. But in 1849 there were no time zones. How confusing was that? But out here, people seemed to rise with the sun and go to bed by the sun. And right now daylight would last longer than at any other time of the year, regardless of what a watch said.

Even soccer and baseball had never tired him out like a long day on a burro. He guessed it was as much stress as physical exercise. As soon as he could after eating, he stretched out on a blanket on the ground and fell into a deep sleep.

Next morning, Zane was so sore he could hardly walk around. His buttocks and inner thighs in particular.

"Saddle sore," Tom said, when Zane mentioned it privately. "You'll harden up to it in a couple days. Meanwhile, try sitting on one cheek and then the other. Me and Huck are right tender in them parts ourselves, not being brung up to horseback ridin'."

"Becky must be a lot tougher than I am," Zane observed. "She never mentioned being sore."

"You think a girl's gonna to tell you somethin' like that?" Tom was scornful. "She'd die of embarrassment."

Another lesson of the nineteenth century. Yet, after breakfast, he gained a measure of satisfaction when he noticed Becky accepting the invitation of one of the women to ride on the seat of their family's wagon — allegedly for talk and company. Becky's pinto was trailed along behind.

An hour after the six wagons were on the trail, Zane reined up and dismounted. "Let's you and I both get a little relief," he muttered to his burro as he moved ahead to walk and lead the animal.

For the next several days, the routine was the same. Zane did, indeed, toughen up to the saddle and the trail.

They struck the Platte River and the trail turned to follow it. Zane thought there was a major highway along this route in his time, but couldn't recall the number of the interstate. When he'd traveled any distance from his home in Delaware with his parents, they'd always flown, so he didn't have the intimate familiarity with the country as travelers of this slower era.

In spite of the fact that he was trying to gain weight, he found himself growing leaner, his muscles hardening and the skin of his face and hands weathering darker. The incessant prairie wind kept blowing off his straw hat, so he borrowed a strip of rawhide from one of the men and fashioned a cord to tie under his chin and keep his hat in place. Lacking any dark glasses to protect his eyes from blowing dust, he took to wearing his prescription glasses part of the time. He didn't have to look at himself, but he must have presented a rather ludicrous sight, he thought. He wondered what his friends back home would think if they saw him now, perched atop a burro, wearing a straw hat and horn-rimmed glasses, pants with one suspender and a belt. All he needed now to look completely ridiculous, he thought, was a parasol to hold over his head to resemble one of the illustrations he'd seen in Mark Twain's book *The Innocents Abroad*.

For variety, Tom and Huck sometimes rode back and forth alongside the wagons, but Zane kept to the rear, unsure of his riding skills, usually letting his burro have his head to walk along contentedly, now and then pausing to crop a tasty morsel of grass.

One still moonlit night, Tom, Huck, Zane, Becky, and Jim sat up late around a campfire after the adults in the wagon train had taken to their beds for the night.

Tom, Huck, and Becky had compared notes about their experiences as captives, then speculated on the current whereabouts of the kidnappers.

Then, for a short time they sat staring silently into the fire, with their own thoughts. The lonely silence was punctuated by the yipping of a distant coyote.

At last Tom said, "Zane, should we tell Becky where you came from?"

"Sure. The rest of you know. After what we been through, she has a right to the whole story."

"Zane is from a future time — almost two hundred years from now."

"What?"

The boys related what they had deduced of Zane's origin.

"That's hogwash!" Becky said.

But Tom and Huck persisted, while Zane chipped in what he knew. He even showed her his cell phone and retrieved a snapshot of an airliner he'd forgotten he'd stored in the device. "This here is what replaced balloons for people to fly around in," he told her, simplifying the story. "The main thing we haven't decided is whether the whole world has moved back to 1849, or it's only me," Zane said. "If it's the whole world, like Tom thinks, then none of these future things has happened yet — like wars and such, and my parents and great-great grandparents haven't even been born yet. But if it's only me that came back, my folks will be wondering where I went — *unless* Providence puts me back into my former life at the exact point where I left it, in which case nobody will even know I've been gone."

The boys grinned at the incredulous look on her face.

"Jim, I think these three been chewing loco weed or they're moonstruck." She stood up, brushing off her skirt. "I'm going to bed before this gets any crazier."

Several nights later, Carrick was unable to find room for his small wagon train down in a hollow near the Platte River. Earlier arrivals had jammed this camping spot with hundreds of wagons that stretched along the river for nearly a mile. So he'd guided his train to higher ground north of the river and circled them up to form a dry camp.

As he squatted by the fire that night, sipping coffee, he seemed more concerned than Zane had seen him before.

"This is worse than the roads back east near the cities," Carrick remarked to one of the men next to him. "The trail is being overwhelmed by hundreds of wagons and thousands of animals. The water is being polluted, and every usable stick of wood has been stripped off the cottonwoods along the stream. No grass within miles. Looks like a plague of locusts has been through here."

He had already given orders for everyone on the train — men, women, and children — to begin picking up dried dung, buffalo chips and cow chips, for fuel and toss them into squares of canvas slung beneath the wagons.

"Jacob, I'm putting you in charge of the train tomorrow," Carrick said to the man finishing his meal beside him. "I want to make a foray off to the north to see if I can find some better forage. If so, we'll fill our water barrels and break away from the main trail for a few days."

He stood and stretched. "I'm turning in." He looked across the fire. "Boys, if you want to ride with me in the morning on a scout, you might see some of the country. I'll take my rifle and maybe if I bag a deer or antelope — even a buffalo — we can all have some fresh meat and then smoke the rest for later."

Tom and Huck looked at each other and grinned so wide their faces nearly split. Except for their scabbed wrists, they had apparently recovered from their earlier ordeal.

That night, Zane was kept awake until late by the mournful crying of coyotes. Or was it wolves? He'd never heard either so didn't know the difference. What a lonely sound in the still light of the moon!

A northwesterly breeze kept any dew from forming that night. It made for comfortable, dry sleeping under the stars and wagons, but lack of rain was becoming a concern. "It's not normally this dry this early this far east," Carrick summed up the next morning as they saddled up. "Keep an eye open for any streams or springs. In this open country you can spot clumps of green trees from quite a distance. That indicates there's water down in the swales."

All of them except Becky had volunteered to go on this scout. She had struck up a friendship with a young wife on one of the wagons, and preferred to stay close.

Tom seemed to thirst for adventure more than the animals thirsted for water. To him, adventure was better than fresh-baked rhubarb pie.

Huck was pretty much game for any new enterprise.

And Zane and Jim went along to break the monotony and see something for a few hours besides plodding oxen, creaking wagons, and dust.

They filled their canteens and hung them on the saddles and stuffed some strips of dried, smoked beef and buffalo hump into their saddlebags to eat. Zane thought these withered, dark strips of jerked meat looked like licorice.

The sun was topping the eastern horizon when they rode away, following the river for a ways and then striking north and west.

With his feet firmly in the stirrups, knees steadying himself and a good grip on the reins, Zane was beginning to feel more confident about his riding.

Besides Carrick, who had a single shot rifle and a Colt revolver, Jim was the only one carrying a firearm — the small, .31 caliber Baby Dragoon. But, in this wide-open country where he could spot danger from a long way off, and with the seasoned frontiersman nearby, Zane had no qualms about being completely defenseless.

Only a mile from the wagon train, they startled a big brownish bird that flapped up heavily from the deep grass, a jackrabbit in its talons. After a short distance, the bird dropped its heavy prey and, thrusting mightily with a six-foot wingspan, began to gain altitude.

"Wow!" Zane breathed.

"A golden eagle," Carrick said. "Lotsa small critters out here they prey on. A magnificent bird."

They'd been riding about two hours and the view of the gently rolling plain gave Zane the feeling that a person could ride on and on forever until he fell off the edge of the world.

They topped a slight rise and Carrick drew up so they could take a breather and have a look around. The guide pulled out his telescopic spyglass and began to scan the countryside around.

While his burro put his head down to graze, Zane stood in his stirrups and breathed deeply of the fresh prairie wind. No farmhouses, no roads, no fences, no telephone poles or railroad tracks, no corn-fields or waving wheat — only thigh-high grass rustling quietly in the great distances.

When he glanced at the sky, there were no jet contrails. But a slight movement from the south caught his eye. Something coming toward them across the sky. As it approached, he saw it was a dense flock of birds, flying close together, darting like swallows with similar sharply defined wings. He gasped as they came on, massive numbers of them veering and swooping as one, less than a hundred feet above the ground. The whooshing of thousands of wings startled him more than the sudden thunder of quail taking flight.

He cringed as they swooped overhead. The dense flock came on and on. He slid out of the saddle and stood transfixed, gripping the saddle horn as if to hold himself in place while the unending feathered mass flowed overhead, causing vertigo while he watched it.

More than five minutes passed and still they came like a seething, flowing river in the sky. At length they passed and he let out a deep breath when the flock flew away to the northeast like the passing of a storm cloud. A few feathers drifted down in their wake.

"What was *that*?" he managed to gasp.

"Only a small flock of passenger pigeons," Carrick said.

"A *small* flock?"

"Oh, yeah. I've seen 'em take an hour or two to pass in flights so thick they block out the sun like an eclipse."

Zane could hardly believe it. "Passenger

pigeons became extinct long before I was born," he said in a low voice to Tom and Huck so Carrick couldn't hear.

"Can't be," Tom said with finality. "They's so many they could fill the whole world. They's so thick, hunters don't bother shooting them; they catch 'em in nets. Use the meat to feed the slaves."

"They *are* extinct in my time," Zane insisted, still shaken by the realization that such a thing could happen in only a couple of generations. "There is not even one left alive."

"I'll go along with most o' what you say about your time, but that's a real stretcher," Tom said.

"Well, let me tell you another fact you may or may not believe," Zane continued, somewhat riled that he was being called a liar. "The United States recently had a black president who served for two terms."

Jim looked interested. But Tom and Huck regarded Zane with disdainful looks. "No such thing!" Tom stated.

"Is that the brass-bound truth?" Huck wondered. "If Pap warn't already dead and gone, that kinda news would kill him sure."

CHAPTER 25

"Zane, if you think those pigeons were something, come take a look at this," Carrick said.

Zane mounted his burro and rode to the guide's side, taking the spyglass from Carrick.

"Look off to the southwest there," Carrick pointed.

When he focused the glass, he saw in the distance what looked like a brown caterpillar. Then it seemed to resolve itself into a fuzzy, crawling carpet. He took the telescope away from his eye and looked again. Only a dark line.

Then he used the glass again, and suddenly gasped. "Buffalo!"

"Yep," Carrick said, taking the telescope and handing it over for the others to have a look. "A good-sized herd from the look of it. Hope a couple hunters from the train are out far enough to spot them. All the trains

304

could use some fresh meat."

"There must be thousands of them," Zane said.

"Very likely," Carrick said, "though all the traffic along the Oregon Trail has disrupted their migration routes. They don't seem as plentiful as they did five or six years ago."

"I reckon you're gonna tell us all the buffalo are wiped out in your time," Tom scoffed.

"No, we still have them, but they were barely saved from extinction when only a few hundred were left. I've read there was such fearful slaughter by the late 1870s a hunter had to go for many days out here before he could spot maybe a half dozen animals."

"Another of your stretchers, I'll be bound," Tom said.

"Only twenty or thirty years from now, you remember what I said," Zane warned, feeling like an Old Testament prophet.

"Why would anyone shoot all the buffalo?" Huck asked. "They's enough buffalo meat out there to feed the whole country for the next thousand years."

"For the hides," Zane said. "And to take away everything the Plains Indians depend on so they could be conquered." He remembered these sad tales from his American history classes.

Tom and Huck looked at him and then shook their heads in disbelief.

"Young man, I don't know if you're stringing these boys along, or you're just guessing about the future," Carrick said to Zane. "But I could envision that happening. The Plains tribes *do* depend on the buffalo to live. No resource, living or otherwise, is limitless. I've already lived long enough to see beaver and mink and river otter decline from trapping."

While they were talking the sun had slid under a cloud and the wind began gusting, bending up Carrick's hat brim. Zane noticed the scout watching the sky to the west. It had turned ominously dark.

"Let's go, boys," Carrick said, neckreining his horse. "She's gonna come on to storm in a little while and we don't want to be caught out in the open. See the greenish tint to that black cloud, low down? That's a sure enough sign there's hail, so it ain't nothing to fool around with."

They urged their mounts to a trot. The wagon train was miles to the south, but Zane realized the scout was leading them toward a clump of cottonwoods in a creek bottom to shelter from the coming blast.

They'd only ridden a couple hundred

yards when a cluster of Indian horsemen swept out of the hollow and reined up, eighty yards in front.

Zane caught his breath and his heart skipped a beat or three. Both parties halted, eyeing each other from a safe distance. Sudden fear froze Zane for several seconds. He gripped the reins of his burro.

"Oh, no!" Tom breathed.

Zane took a deep breath, trying to calm himself while his eyes took in this apparition. There were a dozen or fifteen warriors, naked except for breechclouts, bronze skin painted with red, blue, and yellow markings, eagle feathers waving in their long, black hair, ponies decorated with various symbols.

The leader out front wore a long headdress of eagle feathers that hung down his back, ruffling in the wind. Each rider was armed with a bow and a quiver full of arrows with knives at their waists.

Scared as he was, Zane was thrilled at the sight. Silhouetted against the black sky, wind blowing their feathers, the brightly painted ponies sidling and tossing their manes, these Indians were the picture of all that was wild and free in the world.

"Hold steady, boys," Carrick said, raising his hand, palm outward in a symbol of greeting. "It's a Sioux war party."

"Not a hunting party?" Tom's voice quavered a bit.

"They're painted for battle. They'd likely have some of their women along if they were hunting buffalo."

"Oh."

With yips and yells, the Indians swept down into the slight depression and then rode up and surrounded them.

"Keep your hands in sight and don't make any sudden moves," Carrick said. "They look mighty irritated and we're easy pickings. Let's see what they want. Maybe I can parlay our way out of this."

When they rode in tight, Zane caught a musky odor, saw the paint streaked with sweat, and heard their grunts as they inspected the little party.

Zane glanced over at Jim. His eyes were wide under the brim of his flop hat.

With guttural bursts, the Sioux began commenting to one another.

The leader in the long headdress stopped in front of Carrick, and the two began to sign with their hands.

"You speak Sioux?" Tom asked in a tight voice.

"Only a little," Carrick muttered. "But most tribes know sign language."

From the vigorous gestures, pointing, and an explosive word now and then, Zane gathered the head Indian was aggravated about something.

While he had a chance, Zane studied the features of these men. What were they thinking? What was happening behind those dark eyes? With a jolt he realized they were humans, like he was — they weren't animals or some kind of subspecies. Their skin was darker than his and they all had strong features and no whiskers, but differed from one another in looks as their own little group did.

One rider edged his pony forward, reached over, and snatched off Zane's glasses, looking at them curiously, then put them on. When the lenses distorted his view, he yanked them off in wonder as if they were magic. Zane had to choke back a laugh. The Sioux decided to keep the eyewear and shoved them into a pouch at his waist.

Another warrior had ridden up to Jim and touched the big man with a short spear he carried. Then he grew bolder, reached out a hand and rubbed the black arm, and looked at his fingers to see if the charcoal had come off. Maybe he'd win an extra coup feather for his bravery, Zane thought. In spite of their fearsome aspect, they were almost like children.

Carrick and the leader were still signing and pointing.

"They're not sure what to make of us," Carrick said quietly. "Especially Jim."

"Looks like they want a fight," Huck said. "Worse than the Grangerfords and the Shepherdsons. Hope they got a better reason."

"It's the usual thing," Carrick said. "They're alarmed because the whites — as many as leaves on the trees — are invading Sioux land. Whites come in swarms, like locusts, chopping down the trees, stripping off the grass, fouling the streams with dead animals, bringing strange sickness — cholera and measles." He shook his head. "The whites are too many to fight, but the Sioux and their allies will steal our horses and guns and food and kill as many as they can — usually picking off stragglers like us. That's about the gist of it."

Zane swallowed hard. Stragglers?

The Indian leader began speaking again, gesturing and pointing.

"They're taking us to their camp," Carrick said. "Ride along peaceful and don't talk. We'll have to play this by ear."

With the Indians surrounding them, Tom, Huck, Jim, Zane, and Carrick were herded

310

to the west at a trot.

Well, if Tom had wanted to go adventuring amongst the Injuns, his wish had been fulfilled in abundance, Zane thought. Sometimes imagining an adventure was a lot safer than the real thing. Tom had always insisted Indians were honest and honorable and brave and noble. Where he'd absorbed this idea, Zane guessed from Tom's conversation, was from reading romantic novels.

After two miles they reached a camp that turned out to be a cluster of fifteen hide tepees pitched on flat ground 200 yards from a small creek. The camp was inhabited by numerous women, children, and barking dogs. Zane wondered if the dogs were for guarding or for food in lean times.

They were directed to dismount and did. The women were apparently preparing to break camp in the face of the approaching storm, but dropped what they were doing and surrounded the little party, poking and prodding them as if they were livestock up for auction. The smaller children looked on, wide-eyed, at these strangers.

Everyone seemed to be talking at once and Zane wished he could understand the language.

A couple of the younger women were running their hands over Jim and smiling, much to his obvious discomfort.

A tent flap was thrown back and an older man emerged, white hair in long braids that hung down on each side of a face that resembled a brown, dry lake bed with hundreds of cracks and creases.

"Running Wolf!" Carrick cried, opening his arms wide at the sight of this ancient.

"Carrick!" the man answered taking the scout by the shoulders.

"It is many moons," Carrick said. "Are you well?"

"Old," the elder said, stating the obvious, and almost smiled.

"Running Wolf and I knew each other in the old days when I was working for the American Fur Company," Carrick explained. "He was a great and wise warrior."

"Old now," the Indian repeated. "We must feast," Running Wolf decided, then said something to the warriors and to the women.

But an older woman pointed at the approaching black cloud and apparently told him the feast would have to wait. An artificial early twilight was creeping over the plains.

Zane took a hard look in that direction. Far off, he could barely make out a dark funnel. It appeared to be scarcely moving, twisting, but probing the earth from under the massive greenish cloud. In the clear air of this wide-open country, things that appeared to be twenty miles away were as likely to be fifty.

But if Zane had spied that distant tornado in his other world, he would have been diving for the nearest ditch or cave or cellar.

"Must show you," Running Wolf said, ignoring the protesting woman, and taking Carrick by the arm. "Your two white men," he began as he led the scout toward the rear of the camp. "They kill Winter Hawk."

Zane and the boys followed.

Between the cluster of tepees and the picket line that held the spare horses, two men were tied, spread-eagled, on a framework of saplings, apparently semiconscious. Their hats were missing, their clothes torn, and their faces streaked with blood.

"We skin," Running Wolf said. "Take scalp. Put fire here." He indicated his chest. He accompanied the halting English with vigorous gestures.

Two women cursed shrilly in Sioux and lashed switches across the faces of the helpless men. Zane guessed these two would provide entertainment before being scalped and roasted alive for the murder of a warrior, and maybe only for being white in

Sioux country. He'd read the Apache exceeded all others for ingenious torture, but the Sioux were not far behind.

"The noble red man," Zane remarked sarcastically to Tom before he remembered that Running Wolf apparently understood and spoke English.

"It be dem!" Jim cried.

"Who?"

The boys leaned closer. The black, drooping mustache, the scruffy reddish brown hair. They weren't in disguise now. It was Weir and Smealey.

CHAPTER 26

"Your two kidnappers?" Carrick asked in a low voice.

"Yes."

"You bring these men into our country," Running Wolf stated, not in such a good humor now.

"No," Carrick said. "They come alone. Very bad men. Steal from these boys." He indicated Tom and Huck, then pointed at the tied men. "They run away."

There was a grumbling among the Sioux crowding around and Zane felt the baleful stares. Were these Indians assuming all white men were the same and should be treated the same? In his own time, many whites made the same assumptions about blacks, Chinese, and Indians. He sensed an undercurrent of resentment that could be taken out on them as well — similar to an inner-city riot about to break out, punishing the innocent with the guilty.

"Don't say nothing, boys," Carrick said, turning away from the sight. "I can understand some o' their talk. A few of them are out for any white blood. Jim might escape it, but we could be roasted right alongside these kidnappers if I don't play this right."

A cold hand clutched at Zane's heart.

Thunder boomed, hardly more than a mile away.

Carrick walked to his horse and opened the saddlebag, pulling out a hefty canvas sack tied with a drawstring.

Was he bribing them with gold? Where was the gold Weir and Smealey had taken?

"My old friend, Running Wolf, has many wives and many children," Carrick said, smoothly, handing the sack to the old man. "Running Wolf has counted many coups in battle and taken many scalps. It is time for him to rest with much honor. Here is something to help soothe the aches in your bones during the moon of popping trees."

While the old Indian's gnarled fingers were fumbling with the drawstring, Carrick said in a low aside to the boys, "It's seven pounds of the best shag tobacco, mixed with latakia and a hefty portion of hemp."

Some of the other Indians were now beginning to lose interest in these proceedings and pay more attention to the coming storm. Many of the women had turned to striking camp, dropping the tepee poles and rolling up the hide coverings.

A gust of wind whipped a cloud of dust across the bare ground, scattering ashes from the cooking fires.

Zane sprang to his burro and took hold of his halter. An Indian had grabbed the reins of Jim's mule and the other loose horses that were whinnying and tossing their heads in alarm.

Carrick was suddenly there. "Okay, let's git out of here. Running Wolf has given us his blessing to leave, and none of these other braves dare cross him."

All five mounted quickly and kicked their animals into motion, although the high-strung horses needed no encouragement and bolted like racehorses.

Jim and Zane were left fifty yards behind, but caught up when Carrick and the boys slowed down over the crest of a hill a half-mile away.

The wind was roaring now, and Carrick shouted something that couldn't be heard, but pointed toward a clump of trees growing near a cutbank in a creek bottom.

They raced for this meager shelter.

As they plunged their mounts down the wash, the rain burst over them and then hailstones began pelting down, bouncing in every direction. The animals were jumping and plunging as the ice stung their hides and heads.

Holding the reins, the men were able to huddle up under the lip of the cutbank and keep the largest ice balls from hitting them.

"We gotta set those men loose!" Huck shouted.

Nobody answered. Darkness had almost fallen. It would be a long wet night. The temperature had plunged at least twenty degrees within minutes.

"Weir and Smealey — we can't let them burn up!" Huck yelled.

"De Injuns got 'em, Huck. Ain't nuffin' we kin do." Jim's voice boomed.

"I have to try."

"Why d'you care?" Tom shouted back. "Look what they did to me and you and Becky. Let the Injuns have 'em."

"Then, if you don't care about them wretches, Tom Sawyer, let's you and me go after the gold," Huck cried.

"Now you're talkin'! I wondered when somebody was gonna mention them bags o' gold."

The roar of hailstones hitting the trees, ground, and rocks was so loud, they had to shout to be heard.

The boys sprang to their horses and vaulted into the saddles. Zane and Jim were a bit slower with their mounts.

As the burro took off, slipping and sliding up the bank after the boys, Zane barely heard Carrick shouting something but paid no mind.

He ducked his head against the slashing ice that was bouncing everywhere, beginning to accumulate on the ground and in the prairie grass. In the rush of excitement, he hardly knew what he was doing or why. The hail stung like thrown gravel, but the straw hat partially protected his head and face. Squinting ahead, he saw Tom and Huck galloping toward the site of the Sioux camp. He twisted in the saddle and looked back. Jim was only thirty yards behind and closing fast.

The deserted camp was less than a mile away. When Zane reined up and leapt off, Tom and Huck were already standing over the two kidnappers, who were still stretched on the willow frame, deserted by their Indian captors.

"Where's our gold?" Tom shouted at them.

They ignored him, trying to turn their faces away from the hail. The sharp ice was beginning to cut the skin of their faces and arms.

319

"Tell us where the gold is and we'll cut you loose," Huck yelled.

"We spent it!" Smealey shot back at them.

"You ain't had time to spend it."

"We lost it in the river," Weir said, spitting a hailstone out of his mouth.

"You wouldn't of come out this far on the trail if you didn't have the gold," Tom shouted. "Tell us where you hid it."

"It ain't on us," Smealey said. "The Injuns took it."

"They took your horses, but never mentioned you had no gold in your saddlebags."

"That's 'cause Injuns don't care about gold, except for jewelry."

Jim had come up by this time, and he pointed his pistol at the two men on the ground. "Dis be yo las' chance."

"Ah! Shooting us would be a blessing," Smealey cried. "I've lost circulation in my arms and I can't hardly breathe."

Tom pushed Jim's gun aside and faced the two. "If you don't tell us where you hid the gold, we'll mount up and ride off and let the Injuns have you. They'll come back as soon as the storm passes and scalp you and build a fire on your chests, like they said they was gonna do. You want your livers and lungs and stuff roasted? Likely take a long time to die that way."

That produced looks of fear on both men's faces.

"Okay, to Hell with the gold!" Weir cried, blinking through the wet black hair hanging in his face. "We saw the Injuns comin' for us and we stashed it over yonder in that creek bed."

"Where, exactly?"

"I dunno. Couple hundred yards south o' here."

"It's stuffed up under a tree on the bank where the water washed out the roots," Smealey added. "Now, cut us loose, please! I'm beggin' you."

Tom and Huck looked at each other. "I reckon they're tellin' truth," Huck said.

"Iffen I was in their britches, I would too," Tom said, pulling out his Barlow knife and opening it. "Keep your gun on 'em, Jim."

Tom slashed the wet rawhide thongs that were cutting into the men's wrists and bare ankles.

The boys jumped back, ready for anything, but the kidnappers could barely move their arms and legs, and only rolled over off the sapling frame, groaning, trying to ease their stiffened limbs into some kind of motion.

"You're on your own," Tom said. "You'd best be footin' it outa here. You ain't got any boots or horses, but I'd be for runnin'."

Zane pulled several limp strips of smoked jerky from his pocket and tossed them to the men. "Here's some food, and there's plenty rainwater. Follow that crick downstream a few miles and you'll come to the Platte."

"Yeah," Huck said. "You're sure to fetch up with a wagon train that'll take you in."

Jim and the boys mounted up and, with a last look at the two men who were now staggering around barefoot in ankle-deep hailstones, rode off toward the creek.

The hail had eased off, but it was raining a cold rain when the four guided their mounts down into the creek bed. Water was already beginning to rise as they walked their animals along downstream looking at the trees along the bank for the hiding place.

After an anxious five minutes, Tom pointed ahead. "There! That giant cottonwood."

Tom and Huck leapt off their horses and splashed up to the projecting gnarled roots, exposed by the caving bank.

Tom dropped to his knees, ignoring the slippery mud, and thrust both arms in under the leaning tree.

"Here it is!" he shouted, pulling out a soggy canvas bag. "Both of them." He thrust one heavy bag at Huck.

"Yaayy!!" Zane shouted.

Even Jim was grinning.

It grew suddenly darker and an ominous roar reached Zane's ears. Alarmed, he slid out of the saddle, holding tight to the bridle.

Jim's mule was plunging in panic.

Through the trees Zane glimpsed a huge, black funnel bearing down on them, roaring like an out-of-control freight train, tearing up the ground, bushes and trees flying in every direction.

"Down!" Zane yelled, letting go of the burro and diving under the lip of the bank. The others were there a second later.

It was over so fast, Zane could never recall what happened.

Stunned, Zane and the boys rose from their position a minute later, and looked at the receding funnel ripping a path across the grassland toward the northeast.

A fifty-yard-wide swath had been cut in the trees lining the creek. Splintered trees, rocks, and limbs lay everywhere.

Zane's heart was pounding and he felt weak. He sat down on a rock to catch his breath.

Tom and Huck climbed the bank and looked back toward the deserted Sioux camp.

Jim and Zane joined them a minute later.

"Dey be gone, Huck," Jim said, scanning the empty landscape.

"We give 'em a chance," Huck said. "I reckon Providence had other plans."

"Providence, your granny!" Tom snorted as they went back to retrieve their scattered mounts. "Them two are survivors. They'll turn up again, you can bet on it — and they'll be up to some mischief or other."

By the time they'd gathered their uninjured animals, and mounted up, Zane saw Carrick galloping toward them.

"Thank God you're all right," he said, reining up. His buckskins were plastered to him by the rain, but he was grinning. "When we make camp and dry out, I want to hear your story."

Chapter 27

Five days later, Becky, Jim, Tom, Huck, and Zane were standing in front of the sutler's store at Fort Kearny.

Hundreds of wagons were arriving and departing along the trail nearby, coming and going from the rustic fort that was only a small cluster of buildings and warehouses.

Andre Carrick's wagon train was preparing to pull out and continue along the trail to the west. The scout came out of the store and paused to tell them goodbye.

He yanked off his gloves and held out his hand to each of them in turn. "I wish all of you were continuing on west with us," he said. "It's been quite an adventure so far, having you along."

"Thanks. Maybe next year."

"I hope my father has received word by now that I'm all right," Becky said, "but I do need to start home."

"Taken all around, things didn't turn out

325

too badly," the scout said. "You've escaped from your kidnappers and now have most of your ransom back. You young folks are about as resourceful as any I've ever met. Jim, you should be proud of them."

"Yassuh. Ah's mighty proud."

Carrick started to turn away, then stopped. "I talked to the colonel, and he said you could accompany the patrol he's sending back down the trail in the morning toward St. Joe. Only a squad of half dozen soldiers, but they'll make sure you don't have any more trouble, although I can't imagine why you'd need them, except maybe to protect that gold." He paused and looked out at the hundreds of people milling about in the parade ground, which was enclosed by a rectangle of several sod buildings and three or four wooden ones. "This ain't much of a fort, but it's a good re-supply post."

He turned back to them. "The best of luck to you." He waved and strode away.

"Ah 'spect de widow be wonderin' what happen to me," Jim said. "And ah sorta misses de ole place."

"Well, you didn't have to shoot nobody with the widow's gun this trip," Tom said.

"Nossuh. Ah's glad o' dat. She can have it back."

"Zane, you come a long way," Huck said. "You figurin' to head back home?"

Zane had been pondering this very thing for the past few days. "You know, I don't know how I wound up here, so I sure don't know how to go back."

"That's a vexsome question, sure enough."

"So, until Providence shows me the way home, I reckon I'll stick around for a time." He thought of his useless cell phone, which was stowed in his saddlebags.

What would he require to stay on here? New glasses so he could read. He wondered what that Sioux warrior was doing with his old spectacles.

There must be an optometrist in St. Louis who could correct his vision with new glasses and make his eyes ready to see new adventures.

"Well," Tom said, "your parents won't miss you because they haven't been born yet, and neither have your great-grandparents. So I reckon you're free to hang around and we'll all have some rollicksome times. We'll find you a room somers in our village. If you're here come fall, you can go to school with us, though I ain't recommendin' that for winter fun."

"Thanks."

He shook hands with the boys and Jim.

Becky gave him a hug to show he was welcome. A feeling of joy and freedom surged up in Zane like he'd never felt before.

He was confident he'd see his family again. But in only a few weeks, he'd survived some thrilling adventures here, and looked forward to more.

"You reckon there's any such thing as a hamburger around here?" Zane wondered. "I'm starved."

In the years following publication of his two best-known novels, *The Adventures of Tom Sawyer* and *Adventures of Huckleberry Finn*, Mark Twain made several attempts to continue the boys' adventures. But, for whatever reasons, he could never recapture the magic of those first two books.

As an adult, I was thrilled to discover in a university library those later stories — "Tom Sawyer Abroad," "Tom Sawyer, Detective," "Huck Finn and Tom Sawyer Among the Indians," and "Tom Sawyer's Conspiracy." I felt I had unearthed hitherto unknown treasures, but I was disappointed. Those later stories were not all complete, and their writing was not nearly as good as the earlier books I'd read as a twelve year old.

In August, 1948, two months before my eleventh birthday, my father was transferred from Nebraska to Jefferson City, Missouri. There we lived until December, 1952, when the family moved to Arizona. Thus, through nearly four and a half of my formative years, I lived along the Missouri River and roamed the woods and creeks of Mark Twain's home state.

During that time, it was still possible for a boy in Missouri to live much as Tom and Huck had done a century earlier. Of course we had things unknown to Tom and Huck, such as cars and bicycles, electric lights and telephones, radios and movies. On the other hand, we still lacked air-conditioning, television, and such adult-organized sports as Little League baseball. (In those days soccer — so far as we knew — was a game played only in other countries.) And, of course, this was long before satellites, personal computers, cell phones, space travel, and the plethora of electronic devices with which twenty-first-century children are familiar today.

Except for reading (a constant) and board games, there was little to do inside a stuffy house on a nice day. We spent most of our waking hours outdoors using imagination to create games, making many of our own toys — slingshots from tree branches, a five-foot-long wooden boat to launch in the creek — and building a fort in the woods from an empty packing crate, cutting thorn bushes to encircle and defend it. Pretending it was pirate treasure, we buried coins from our collections, then drew an elaborate map to its hiding place. (But we could never find the spot again. The treasure lies there yet.) We explored the town and surrounding countryside on our bikes, played pick-up baseball in the park, climbed trees, made Indian bows, fletching the arrows with chicken feathers, and developed and printed our own black and white film in a basement darkroom. We seined for minnows and crawdads, fished for bluegill and catfish, shelled and ate sunflower seeds, chewed bubble gum, shot BB guns, played kick-the-can, fox-and-the-walnut, and camped out with our dogs in an army surplus pup tent. In winter, we threw ourselves headfirst on sleds, shooting down steep, snowy trails that snaked through the woods. We built snow forts and engaged in epic snowball fights.

Parents were doing whatever grown-ups did then — and that did not include hovering over us to direct our every move, to protect us from danger, to dampen our inventiveness or kill our fun. We were told to go outside and play and be back by suppertime. Parents trusted us to take care of ourselves, and, luckily, we got into trouble only now and then. Much like Mark Twain in his later years, I have great nostalgia for those idyllic times.

Not only was Mark Twain forever captivated by the experiences of his boyhood, he was also intrigued with time travel and historical settings, as demonstrated in such tales as *A Connecticut Yankee in King Arthur's Court, The Prince and the Pauper,* and his unfinished "Mysterious Stranger" stories.

What, then, would a new Tom and Huck adventure be without a time traveler? And what better time traveler than a boy named Zane from the twenty-first century? Was it Chance or Luck that threw this mysterious stranger into their midst to complicate a crisis that arose that very day?

Tom and Huck would have blamed it on Providence.

ABOUT THE AUTHOR

Tim Champlin was born in Fargo, North Dakota, the son of a large-animal veterinarian and a schoolteacher. He grew up in Nebraska, Missouri, and Arizona where he was graduated from St. Mary's High School, Phoenix, before moving to Tennessee.

After earning a BS degree from Middle Tennessee State College, he declined an offer to become a Border Patrol Agent in order to finish work on a Master of Arts in English at Peabody College (now part of Vanderbilt University).

After 39 rejection slips, he sold his first piece of writing in 1971 to *Boating* magazine. The photo article, "Sailing the Mississippi," is a dramatic account of a three-day, 75-mile solo adventure on the Big River from Memphis, Tennessee, to Helena, Arkansas, in a sixteen-foot fiberglass sailboat built from a kit in his basement. His only means of propulsion were river current, sails, and a canoe paddle.

Since then, 38 of his historical novels have been published. Most are set in the Frontier West. A handful of them touch on the Civil War. Others deal with juvenile time travel, a clash between Jack the Ripper and Annie Oakley, the lost Templar treasure, and Mark Twain's hidden recordings.

Besides books, he's written several dozen short stories and nonfiction articles, plus two children's books. One of his most recent books is a nonfiction survey of world-famous author Louis L'Amour and the Wild West.

He has twice been runner-up for a Spur Award from Western Writers of America — once for his novel *The Secret of Lodestar* and once for his short story "Color at Forty-Mile."

Tim is still creating enthralling new tales. Most of his books are available online as ebooks.

In 1994 he retired after working thirty years in the U.S. Civil Service. He and his wife, Ellen, have three grown children and ten grandchildren.

Active in sports all his life, he continues biking, shooting, sailing, and playing tennis.

The employees of Thorndike Press hope you have enjoyed this Large Print book. All our Thorndike, Wheeler, and Kennebec Large Print titles are designed for easy reading, and all our books are made to last. Other Thorndike Press Large Print books are available at your library, through selected bookstores, or directly from us.

For information about titles, please call:
  (800) 223-1244

or visit our Web site at:
  http://gale.cengage.com/thorndike

To share your comments, please write:
  Publisher
  Thorndike Press
  10 Water St., Suite 310
  Waterville, ME 04901